I0531122

LYNTON WALKS ON WATER

WHILE INGRID AND CHANNA DO AN IRISH JIG

BY

J. WAYNE FRYE

Note to university and high school teachers: This book is written in Canadian English, so discrepancies in the spelling of words should be explained to students. In the vocabulary section the Canadian spelling is used, and the definitions are based upon the meaning within the context of this book. It is suggested that a review of the vocabulary precede the reading of each chapter.

LYNTON WALKS ON WATER WHILE INGRID AND CHANNA DO AN IRISH JIG

The Author

Wayne Frye's *Aaron Adams, Girl* series books and *Lynton* adventures have been popular among mystery lovers since first appearing in 2005. He provides satirical political commentary to many Canadian newspapers, and his books on politics have created a great deal of controversy. He has written marketing/advertising textbooks, been a highly successful U.S. university hockey coach, professor, university president and served as a marketing consultant to hockey teams and motion picture companies. He has been cited for his work with inner-city gang children in the Los Angeles area and been active in the anti-globalization movement. He became a Canadian citizen in 2003 and lives in Ladysmith, British Columbia and Cavite, Philippines.

Other Books by J. Wayne Frye
Hockey Mania and the Mystery of Nancy Running Elk
Something Evil in the Darkness at Hopkins House
How Hockey Saved a Jew From the Holocaust:
The Rudi Ball Story
The Catastrophic Calamities of a Village Idiot
Fighting for Justice in the Land of Hypocrisy
Guide to Alternative Education (13 Editions)
Cataclysmic Dreams in Black and White
The Girl Who Stirred up the Whirlwind
The Girl Who Motivated Murder Most Foul
The Girl Who Said Goodbye for the Last Time
Fall From Apocalypse
Advertising Lab Manual
Promotions Workbook
Public Relations Workbook
Advertising Design
Armageddon Now
Worth
When Jesus Came to Jersey as the Son of Thunder
When Jesus Came to Canada to Lead an Indigenous Rebellion
Canadian Angels of Mercy – Nurses in Times of Peril
Points of Rebellion: Aboriginals Who Fought for Justice
Lynton Curls Her Hair
Lynton Buys a Cell-Phone and Hears the Voice of Doom
Chablis: Avenging Angel for the Forgotten in the City of Lost Hope

J. WAYNE FRYE   2

LYNTON WALKS ON WATER WHILE INGRID AND CHANNA DO AN IRISH JIG

TABLE OF CONTENTS

J. WAYNE FRYE

LYNTON WALKS ON WATER WHILE INGRID AND CHANNA DO AN IRISH JIG

To Phyllis Strider Williams: Since the death of my dear Aunt Willa Mae, she is now my most loyal fan in Asheboro, North Carolina. Phyllis was a classmate at Asheboro High School, and though we drifted apart over the years, we reconnected and found that there is no friendship like old friendship. As the two of us age, we fondly remember those wonderful adolescent years when all things seemed possible and when each day was a great adventure.

And a special thanks to Sinclair Lewis from whom I borrowed liberally and whose character Elmer Gantry was the inspiration for Robert Torres and also Charles Laughton whose one foray into directing led to an incredible motion picture that was also inspirational to the formulation of this little ditty.

Copyright 2014 by J. Wayne Frye

All rights reserved. No part of this book or covers may be reproduced or transmitted in any form or by any other means, electronic or mechanical, including photocopying, recording, or by any information storage and retrieval system, without permission from the author.

This is a work of fiction. Any similarity to persons living or dead is coincidental.

Catalogue Number: 2014-2453569

ISBN: 978-1-928183-02-0

Fireside Books – Victoria, British Columbia
Part of the Peninsula Publishing Consortium

J. WAYNE FRYE   4

LYNTON WALKS ON WATER WHILE INGRID AND CHANNA DO AN IRISH JIG

PROLOGUE

THE MIRACLE OF WALKING ON WATER

OK, this will be one of those times when I might really upset a lot of my readers. I know there was only one virgin birth according to Christian beliefs. Well, guess what, not only did ancient history record more than one virgin birth; there are also records of men walking on water, curing lepers, making the blind see and resurrecting the dead. So, as I tell all my readers, "I am an equal opportunity offender." Name me the group and I can probably come up with a way of offending them. I guess it is what I like to call, "making people think rather than just accept everything at face value." Just like the invisible weapons of mass destruction in Iraq that George Bush and his henchmen manufactured, all believers, whether it be in the Bible, the Torah, the Koran, or any other holy book, should realize that religion is a personal matter and, for that reason, it should be left to each individual to decide for himself or herself exactly what to believe. The key is that no one should try to impose their beliefs on another. In a world filled with religious animosity that often leads to wars and unspeakable acts of cruelty in the name of God, we must all be eternally vigilant against pointing the finger of judgmental arrogance at those who might believe differently than we do. As Jesus said, "Let he who is without sin cast the first stone."

If there is a God, he gave us a brain to use, not let atrophy from lack of thought. I have read the Bible cover to cover probably twenty times in my life. I find it a fascinating rendition and retelling of stories written long ago before anyone ever heard of Elijah, Moses, Samson, evil snakes, etc... Any inquiring mind can dig up these stories and see that much of what was told in the Bible is simply a recompilation of stories that had been told for years in ancient civilizations. To put it bluntly, those who wrote the Bible weren't very creative as they relied on ancient stories that they simply retold. This does not mean I question the authenticity of these stories; it just means that I have read the stories elsewhere and they were almost all written in another place, in another time before Jesus came along. It is kind of like a movie franchise Part 1, 2 etc... Jesus may well have performed miracles, but other religions also relate tales of their deities doing those things. Just as it was once said "one man's sin is another man's fun," it could also be said with conviction that "what one deity did in one religion might well have been done by another deity in another religion."

The followers of one religion might think the followers of another religion are going to hell, but my guess is that if there is a heaven somewhere, it will be filled with "good men and women" who are Jewish, Christian, Muslim, Hindu, Buddhist and any other religion or even Atheists who lived a life of love for their fellow man.

This does not mean that I am questioning whether there is a God or not. All I ask of people is to accept the fact that in a world filled with misery, do not add to that misery by judging someone by their religion or their lack of religion. I once had a devout Catholic priest tell me that some of the kindest people he knew were atheists and some of the cruellest were Christians. People should all be judged by the content of their character, not by the deity they pray to every day.

Probably the first account of a virgin birth was Mithras. He was a Persian deity and was also the most worshipped and venerated God in the Roman Empire during the time of Jesus. Hundreds of years before the birth of Jesus, Mithras' virgin birth occurred and a bright star appeared in the heavens lighting the way for three wise men from far away to bring him gifts of gold, myrrh and frankincense.

Unlike Jesus, he was really born on December 25. If the accounts in the Bible are correct, the time of Jesus birth would have been closer to mid-summer, for this is when shepherds would have been "tending their flocks in the field" and the new lambs are born. Before he was crucified by non-believers, Mithras had a last supper with his 12 male disciples. After the crucifixion, his body was laid to rest in a rock tomb; he arose days later and ascended to heaven during the spring (around Passover time). His followers referred to him as "the light of the world" and the "prince of peace."

In addition to Mithras, the following deities were born of a virgin before Jesus: Augustus, Adonis, Korybas, Osirus, Tammuz, Agdistis, Buddha, Krishna, Perseus, Zoroaster, Attis, Dionysus, Romulus and Remus. Buddha was called Redeemer, Savoir, King of Kings, Good Shepherd and

LYNTON WALKS ON WATER WHILE
INGRID AND CHANNA DO AN IRISH JIG

Light of the World. Oh, he was also a skilled carpenter. He raised the dead, gave the blind sight and healed lepers. The others mentioned also were called similar names, performed miracles and some actually walked on water, turned water into wine and fed the multitudes from one loaf of bread.

So, with that in mind, I want to make it clear that I intend no disrespect in this book. All I am doing here is pleading for reflective thought and research into where beliefs originate. I am simply mystified by those who close their minds rather than opening them to exploration. All I am doing is pleading for an open mind. People must be willing to pursue truth. If truth had been pursued when lie after lie took the USA into a needless war in Iraq, how many deaths could have been avoided?

The last words of those men who flew planes into the World Trade Centre were "Allah Akbar" (God is Great). And George Bush's response to that cowardly act was to stand with a Bible in one hand and a bevy of missiles in the other to rain down terror from the skies on a Stone Age country. The American government went even further and locked up people as young as 15 years old in Guantanamo and tortured them– no doubt, with the approval of the God Bush and Cheney worship. Would anyone who believed in a merciful, forgiving God perpetrate acts of terrorism to fight terrorism? How many wars have been fought over religion? Even Hitler thought God was punishing the Jews, not only for the economic morass in which Germany found itself, but also for killing Christ.

People must take the time to study and reflect. It is easier to let someone else do our thinking for us as thinking for oneself involves some effort. Do not take the easy way out, and do not blindly ridicule believers and nonbelievers. Having faith is fine, but respect those who have none, and keep an open mind. Never accept anything just at face value. The same applies to this book. It should not be taken at face value. It should be analyzed and carefully scrutinized for accuracy. I am a very opinionated person who has strong beliefs; consequently, the reader should always question my prejudices.

So, with that bit of philosophical background, let us, with open minds, begin an exciting adventure about a young woman who, along with her two friends, was able to take a stand against evil. And in the process, she managed to walk on water.

LYNTON WALKS ON WATER WHILE INGRID AND CHANNA DO AN IRISH JIG

CHAPTER 1
STAND AGAINST EVIL

In the modern world, far too many people let others do their thinking for them. They want direction and guidance, but fall prey to those who only want to disparage, deprecate, ridicule and point the finger of condemnation. Defining evil is easy for those who see everything as black or white. Unfortunately, the world is not all black and white. It is multi-coloured and there are many shades of grey which means many times there are no definitive answers.

Neglecting the needy is justified by blaming the poor for being poor. It is their fault, because they are lazy according to those who recent their tax dollars being used to lift up and lend assistance to the less fortunate.

Those who do not conform and live an alternate lifestyle are considered abominations by the definers of public morals who think there is only one path that all must follow. Somehow, modern thinking equates Christianity with capitalism, so it is perfectly alright to covet what your neighbour has as that is called ambition, which is part and parcel of an economic system based on greed. Yes, greed is good, because it fuels the economy. The more people want the more people buy; therefore, the more people are employed providing goods and services that allow people to buy happiness. In the world of capitalism, an individual's worth is not judged by the content of his or her character, but by the content of their bank account. A person's worth is not based on good acts, but by how much their bank balance is at the end of the month. Religion itself is often part of this system, as it generates vast income through a variety of means.

Sometimes religion attracts nefarious individuals who are rogues and charlatans, and they use their oratorical and manipulative skills for self-interest. One such man was Robert John Torres, who had the good fortune to sit in a jail cell for two years with a man named Ben Ramirez, who had stolen a large sum of money from the Philippine National Bank in Cavite, Philippines and led provincial police on a wild chase all the way to the resort city of Taal, where his wife and two children lived. There, he made it to his humble home that had been given to his father by the

LYNTON WALKS ON WATER WHILE INGRID AND CHANNA DO AN IRISH JIG

Ferdinand Marcos government during one of its land reform campaigns that took property from the rich and redistributed it to the poor. Marcos was deposed in 1986.

The Philippines, like that great haven of corporate capitalism, the USA, was handed over to corporations to run as they liked. For that reason, every day more and more people slipped into poverty and were denied the necessities of life so a few could enjoy lives of splendorous excess. This, according to Ben, necessitated making sure that his children could have an opportunity for an education so that they could at least have a life with a modicum of security. Thus, he had robbed a bank and now stood with nearly one million pesos (about 25,000 Canadian dollars) in a bag. He had to hide it before the police arrived. It was his wife's duty to keep it hidden and only use it in emergencies. Ben would be in jail for a long time, as those who robbed from a bank were expected to pay a heavy price in years, while the bankers, who robbed people every day through exorbitant interest rates, repossessed homes and put women and children on the streets were not robbers at all. They were just smart business people. Thus, as is normal in societies where greed is rewarded, true justice is never meted out to those at the top of the economic ladder, only to those at the bottom.

The two parents tried frantically to find a place to hide the one million pesos which was made up of neatly bundled 1000 peso bills. Their two children were stoically and quizzically standing nearby crying as they observed their frantic parents. Robert handed his wife the money and said, "Don't tell anyone where it is hidden as this is our children's future. I am going to meet my fate. I love you Alana, take care of the children and make sure they get that money so they can have a good start in life, because nothing is going to change in a country where the politicians forget the poor and cater to the corporations and the rich. I love you!"

Robert kissed Alana, went over to his son Louie and said, "Be a good boy Louie. You are only 9 years old and will be teased by children who say your father is a jailbird. Remember that your father is a man who loves you but was unfortunately born poor. I am sorry you must be burdened with this, but I simply reached the end of my rope. He put his arms around Louie and whispered, "Listen to your sister. She is a wise girl who will always lead you in the right direction."

His daughter, Abby, with tears in her eyes, reached up and let him wrap his warm, loving arms around her little body. She felt warm and safe in his embrace. As she sobbed, he said, "You are going to see to it that your mom and brother are safe." He then turned to Alana and Louie. "All of you quickly hide the money and never reveal its whereabouts to anyone, regardless of how much you might trust them."

Eight year old Abby slowly walked over to the old, worn-out sofa and painstakingly picked up her huge stuffed doll which had most of the stuffing already out of it. She thrust it out to her mom and said, "Put the money in there and quickly sew it up."

Louie and his mom nodded affirmatively at one another and knew that Abby had found the perfect hiding place. The money was quickly stuffed in the large doll and it was stitched up as Ben sat on the sofa, patiently waiting for the police.

LYNTON WALKS ON WATER WHILE INGRID AND CHANNA DO AN IRISH JIG

There is little sympathy from the authorities for those who defy the law, regardless of the circumstances. The police are there to protect the wealthy, not to serve the poor, thought little Abby, as she sat down by her father to await the arrival of the police.

Her adoring father looked over and smiled at her as she held her doll. Suddenly, without having the courtesy to knock, five policemen bolted through the door with guns drawn. A rotund, tall one shouted, "Down on the floor scum, now."

With hands held high, Ben stood up and immediately dropped to the floor face-down. "Don't hurt my family, please."

The rotund one shouted, "Screw your family. Anybody move and you're all dead."

Two policemen moved around behind Ben, and one of them slammed his right foot into his back, causing excruciating pain, as he shouted, "Hands behind your back scumbag, now."

J. WAYNE FRYE   17

LYNTON WALKS ON WATER WHILE INGRID AND CHANNA DO AN IRISH JIG

The other policeman cuffed Ben and then two others crabbed him by the arms and viciously pulled him up. The rotund one shouted "OK, where is the money? Where is it?"

Smiling, Ben replied "I tossed the bag off Taal Bridge."

He moved to Ben, kneed him in the stomach and said, "No you didn't. Where is it?" Then, he took out his billy-club and pounded Ben on the back of the neck several times as he shouted, "The money, the money."

The precocious Abby shouted, "You are more interested in the money than what made my dad steal it. You know what poverty forces people to do in order to survive?"

The rotund one looked over at Alana and said, "Better tell that little brat to shut up, or I'll use this club on her to make her think twice before being disrespectful to authorities."

Alana put her right index finger to her lips, indicating that Abby should be quiet. Yet, Abby wasn't through letting the law enforcement officers have a piece of her mind as she said, "If I had enough money to afford a cell-phone, I'd take a video of your abuse of my father and post it on YouTube, so the whole world could see how you treat prisoners."

Now, thoroughly frustrated, the rotund policeman signalled for two officers to take Ben outside, as he said to the other two, "Search the place."

Again, the precocious Abby said, "Where's your search warrant?"

Mr. Rotund went over to her, bent over and said, "Little girl, any more out of you and I am going to my car, get the duct tape out of my trunk and tape your mouth shut."

Abby, still not scared, said, "Go ahead you fat slob, and stop for a donut on the way."

Alana again put her index finger to her mouth, as she was almost pleading with Abby to keep quiet as all through the ordeal, Abby clung to her doll while her brother sat quietly on the sofa.

LYNTON WALKS ON WATER WHILE INGRID AND CHANNA DO AN IRISH JIG

After a thorough search of the humble home of the Ramirez family, the police gave up the quest and assumed maybe Ben did actually toss the bag off the Taal Bridge over the gulley coming into town. It was a distinct possibility that he did it as an act of desperation while the police were in hot pursuit. They would go there to make a thorough search. However, when they found nothing, they kept coming back to Ben's home to search again and again, always coming up empty handed, and never thought to wrest the doll from the grasp of Abby, where the money was hidden. Each time the cops came, little Abby had words of wisdom for them like, "Hey, you guys realize you are working for the biggest thieves of all – the bankers. Don't you realize they lose nothing at all as they have insurance to cover their losses? So, actually you are now working for the second biggest thieves in the country – the insurance companies that insure the banks against losses. Don't you realize that you are all representing the oppressors of the people?"

One cop looked at Alana and said, "Why don't you ship your daughter off to Cuba where all the other stupid commies left in the world are?"

LYNTON WALKS ON WATER WHILE INGRID AND CHANNA DO AN IRISH JIG

About a month later, as justice is swift when the poor are arrested but moves along like a turtle when it is the rich being prosecuted, the judge put Abby on the witness stand to ask her where the money was. She smiled and said, "I don't know, and if I did, I wouldn't tell, because the bank already has been paid by the insurance company, and the insurance company will just cover its loss by raising premiums. I may be a child, but I know the way of the world judge."

The judge laughed at her precociousness and bid the trial continue. It did for about two more days and the jury came back with a unanimous verdict of guilty and Ben, a week later, was sentenced to 25 years in prison.

That doll became Abby's constant companion, even as she sat with her mother in the courtroom watching her father being sentenced. She knew that recovering the money might take a year or two off his sentence, but she had made a promise to her father not to reveal the money's whereabouts. The promise was something she, her brother and her mother were going to keep, because it was what her father wanted.

LYNTON WALKS ON WATER WHILE INGRID AND CHANNA DO AN IRISH JIG

Now, while all this was going on, a young lady named Lynton Viñas (pronounced Veen-yes), who had struggled valiantly through hardships to become a somewhat successful entertainer in shopping malls, singing and dancing her way to adulation from many fans who genuinely appreciated her talent, and operating a successful cosmetics business and a chain of beauty salons, was busy preparing for a show she was putting on at a Shopping Mall in Dasmarinas City, which was about one and one-half hours from Manila. Her featured performers were herself, along with her friends Channa and Ingrid. Readers may recognize the names from two previous Lynton adventures by Wayne Frye: *Lynton Curls Her Hair* and *Lynton Buys a New Cell-Phone*.

On the day of Ben Ramirez's sentencing in a nearby courtroom, afterward, Alana thought bringing Louie and Abby to see the mall show might get their minds off what had just happened to their father. It is often said that providence intervenes in people's lives at opportune times No doubt; Lynton performing that day was certainly a propitious event that was indeed a forerunner for what would follow.

LYNTON WALKS ON WATER WHILE INGRID AND CHANNA DO AN IRISH JIG

Lynton's life had not been one of ease. She had struggled to lift herself out of poverty, and done it through grit and determination. However, she had never taken on an air of arrogance and always reached out with compassion to people whom she saw as less fortunate than she was.

She was the first of five children born to her mom and dad who were poor farmers in a rural area of the Philippines. Life was tough, and Lynton, as the eldest, was looked up to by her siblings. This book is not a biography of Lynton Viñas, but in order to understand the relationship that developed between her and Abby, we must have some rudimentary knowledge of her background as; although there was a great age difference between them, Lynton would see in young Abby almost a carbon copy of herself at the age of 8.

Life on a farm for a young girl can often be grueling. In fact, it was so difficult to eke out a living that the family finally gave up and moved to the city of Cavite, south of Manila. Upset with watching her mom and dad struggle to put food on the table, Lynton decided to strike out on her own to relieve the family from the burden of providing for

LYNTON WALKS ON WATER WHILE INGRID AND CHANNA DO AN IRISH JIG

her. At the age of 12 she went to Manila, where she lived on the streets for two years, earning enough money by selling fruits and vegetables and being a parking lot attendant to feed herself and pay for her private schooling. Eventually, she returned to Cavite, where she went to high school and met a young woman named Ingrid, who became her friend and confidant. Life in their poor neighborhood could often be very tough, so at age 14 the girls joined a gang. Now, we are all told how gangs are bad, but sometimes necessity is the mother of invention. In other words, in order to protect themselves from harassment, they joined a gang which provided them with safety to, from and in school.

By the time they were 16, the girls were independent and so self-assured that they no longer needed the protection of the gang as they both became fearless when standing up for themselves. Now, at 5:2 and 45 kilos (about 100 pounds), Lynton was certainly not an imposing figure, but when she was 16 and starting her senior year, as she and Ingrid were leaving school on the first day, she did something that forever branded her as an individual with whom one simply did not want to tangle.

J. WAYNE FRYE   24

LYNTON WALKS ON WATER WHILE INGRID AND CHANNA DO AN IRISH JIG

As they were leaving school that day, three boys came up to them. One of them said, "You Lynton Viñas are so poor you eat cereal with a fork to save milk. How about we give you 10 pesos for a kiss and you can go to McDonald's and see if you can buy a Big Mac on layaway."

As the three boys burst out in laughter while on-lookers gathered around to join them in the gaiety, Lynton smiled, cocked her head to the left, winked at the boy and replied, "Sammy, you are so stupid you probably go to the beach to surf the internet."

Not to be outdone by Lynton, Sammy replied, "You are so poor you only have two channels on your television, on and off."

The crowd around them began to get larger by the minute, as Lynton, not too be outdone said, "Sammy, you are so stupid that you probably go to the library to find Facebook."

The crowd roared with laughter, but Sammy refused to quit. "Lynton, you are so poor you wave around a Popsicle and call it air conditioning. You are so poor you would probably wrestle a squirrel for a nut."

As the crowd roared, Lynton did not miss a beat. "You are so stupid you talk to an envelope to send voice mail. You are so stupid you would take a ruler to bed to see how long you slept."

That was it, Sammy, embarrassed by the laughter as Lynton refused to cower before him, raised his fist in preparation to hit her. Lynton, as he was bringing his right fist downward toward her face, pivoted to the right and the blow glanced off her shoulder. She moved to Sammy's left side and shoved him to the ground. The other two boys came at her. Ingrid stopped one with a well placed kick where all boys can be hurt the most. The other one was met with a knee to his stomach by the diminutive Lynton. He crumbled to the ground just as Sammy was back on his feet, now coming at Lynton as the crowd backed off and observed the mêlée in disbelief. These were the three toughest boys in the school and little Lynton, and the only slightly bigger Ingrid were not backing down from the psychological and physical confrontation.

LYNTON WALKS ON WATER WHILE
INGRID AND CHANNA DO AN IRISH JIG

As Sammy, fists balled up and rage etched on his face, furiously came at Lynton, she balled up her right fist and hit him so hard on his left cheek that he immediately fell to the ground from the force of the blow. As he lay there, Lynton put her right foot on his chest rendering him with fear that she might push harder on him and crack his ribs. She said "Jerk, next time pick on somebody your own size."

The crowd was laughing almost uncontrollably now as the extremely small Lynton took her foot off his chest and the other two boys continued to writhe in pain as they lay on the ground. The two girls gave each other the high five, and as the crowd applauded, they walked defiantly and proudly away.

Ironically, Sammy, so immensely impressed with Lynton's courage, over time, gradually became good friends with her, and she was actually able to help him become a much nicer person and put his bully nature behind him. In fact, Sammy wound up working for Lynton as her stage manager for the performances she put on in malls all over the Philippines.

LYNTON WALKS ON WATER WHILE INGRID AND CHANNA DO AN IRISH JIG

So, as Lynton prepared for the performance at SM Mall in Dasmarinas City, little Abby was wandering around the seating area while her mother and brother were in a nearby store. She noticed Lynton on stage setting up and went to her, stood there and stared. Lynton smiled and said, "So, what's your name?"

"I'm Abby. I have seen you on television. You are Lynton. My mommy says we can watch the show today. You are a pretty girl."

Impressed with the openness of the young girl, Lynton said, "Well, tell your mommy that I am reserving front row seats for you."

"Well, there's my brother, too," said Abby as she artfully let a smile creep across her lips.

Smiling, Lynton motioned for Sammy to come over. She introduced him to Abby and said, "Please put a reserved sticker on three seats in front for Abby, her mom and brother and tell security to escort them down front when they get here."

LYNTON WALKS ON WATER WHILE
INGRID AND CHANNA DO AN IRISH JIG

Abby, with a huge grin, said, "You are nice Lynton. Thank you very much."

"Well, you are welcome Abby. I will see you later, as I must get ready for my performance now."

Lynton went back stage and her friends and co-performers, Channa and Ingrid, were beginning to put on their costumes. Ingrid and Channa were beautiful women, and, along with Lynton, they formed a trio that was mesmerizing to watch perform. The three women, accompanied by a four piece band, always attracted shoppers to malls to see them perform. For awhile they had been struggling, but when Lynton fell in love with Wayne Frye, a former promoter of concerts in the North-eastern USA, she not only got a lover, but she wound up with a man who had once been called the marketing genius by the *Los Angeles Times*. Before Wayne took over their management, they had charged people 100 pesos (about $1.25 cents Canadian) to watch their incredible performances, but Wayne came up with the idea of promoting the girls to the malls, who would pay them to give free performances to attract customers. This new approach was getting them more bookings than they had ever had before.

Wayne was currently back in Canada on business, so Lynton busied herself with mall engagements to take her mind off missing him. However, this particular engagement at the SM Mall, where she met little Abby Ramirez, would be a most unusual event that would lead to Lynton getting involved with an incredibly evil man who had nefarious intentions when it came to little Abby, her brother and mom.

Many months went by and Abby, along with her mom and brother, were forced to leave their humble home when they missed two payments on the mortgage, as like most poor people, they were not even afforded the courtesy of a roof over their heads by a government or a ruthless corporation that was only concerned with the bottom line.

Being true to her promise, Alana never considered for a moment using any of the funds Ben had stolen, as she had solemnly promised that it would be saved for a university education for the children. So, the family was reduced to living in the streets until Alana was able to pay the back mortgage payments and return to their home. While government officials rode by in luxuriously appointed chauffeured limousines sipping their morning lattes on the way to their lavishly furnished air conditioned offices provided at taxpayer expense, the nearly destitute Ramirez family and millions of others like them, wondered where their next bowl of rice would come from. Thus is the way of a world where greed rules supreme.

While all this was going on, Lynton, Channa and Ingrid were continuing their careers as mall performers, unaware of the sad state of affairs that little Abby found herself in. Lynton had first hand experience living on the streets, but Channa and Ingrid had come from more affluent families, so they did not suffer poverty's pinch as children. However, all three of these women were well-known for their compassion. In fact, so legendary was Lynton's compassion that she was often chastised by friends for going overboard in her generosity. Most of those who criticized her were of the Christian faith, so she would always tell them, "Remember Jesus told the wealthy man that he should give all he has to the poor."

LYNTON WALKS ON WATER WHILE INGRID AND CHANNA DO AN IRISH JIG

Channa, incredibly beautiful, but ever the practical woman, would sarcastically interject, "Yeah, and when Jesus told him that, the rich man turned away from him. Rich people pick and chose the parts of the Bible they want to follow. It is more convenient for their bank account that way."

Smiling, Lynton replied, "Yes, the rich have a habit of loving Jesus, as long as it doesn't cost them too much, or they don't have to follow that plea to give all they have to the poor. I am sure they prefer the Jesus quote about the poor we have always as justification for ignoring their plight. So, your point is well taken Ms. Channa, I will try to temper my compassion so that I don't wind up in the poor house."

Channa was a woman who was very easy on the eyes, and had won many beauty pageants over the years. In fact, her shapely frame could have been the inspiration for a song by a famous singer that was refined by none other than Wayne Frye.

Oh man, oh man, check her out.

LYNTON WALKS ON WATER WHILE INGRID AND CHANNA DO AN IRISH JIG

That girl is really hot.
Check her out. Check her out.
I want to give her what I got.

Hey girl, hey girl, you can't be lame.
Ummm! You have a nice brown frame.
I bet all men tell you the same.
They all love that sweet brown frame.

Hey girl, I have seen you around.
Things are hot when you hit town.
You probably hum a sweet sound.
Put that gorgeous frame in a gown.

I would gladly put you on a throne.
Please don't leave me alone.
Come on, grab up a chair
And come over here.

Get solid with me.
Come on, can't you see.
I will whisper your name
Looking at your fine brown frame.

J. WAYNE FRYE   33

LYNTON WALKS ON WATER WHILE INGRID AND CHANNA DO AN IRISH JIG

Baby I want to scream at what I have seen.
Please don't ignore me. Don't be mean.
Your beauty must give you fame
With that fine brown frame!

Please baby, come over here.
You don't have anything to fear.
I will put you up on a throne.
I can't leave that fine brown frame alone.

Other women may feel like silk
But they are as white as milk.
You, baby light my flame
With that fine brown frame.

Beauty is far too often physically ascribed. In Channa's case, the beauty was more than skin deep. Deep within was a kind heart that beat with a rhythm of peace and tranquility that reached out with compassion for all. Yet, the physical attributes could not be denied. The long, full, flowing, straight dark brown hair glistened like a diamond sparkling under a bright light. Her forehead was smooth and wrinkle free. The sparkling eyes darted about like a flash of lighting ready to strike, and the glasses she often wore added a touch of intellectual charm. Her nose was slightly raised rather than Asian flat, and made you want to plant a sweet kiss on its tip. And her lips, though a bit thin, when licked by her darting tongue, made men want to taste their sweetness. Ah, and the shoulders were thrown back with pride and her posture a fastidious endorsement of her prim and proper manner that made you realize this was a woman with depth of character. Oh, and the bosom that heaved up and down in the tight-fitting blouses she wore were just an inducement to scan further down at the taunt waistline and finally the tapering legs that were silky smooth and led to perfectly formed dainty feet that usually peeked out from high fashion flip-flops. Yes, the song Wayne wrote was very apropos. This girl had one fine brown frame.

Ingrid, like Channa, a bit tall for a Filipino woman, had a fine frame that accentuated all her womanly assets. Her hair, which she often wore, like Channa, pulled back in a pony tail, was dark golden brown and the tail of it provocatively swayed from side-to-side as she strode about with a sublime confident manner, shoulders reared back, chest stuck out and a seductive sway to her hips. Her dark, penetrating eyes seemed to glow like two beacons in the night, lighting the way to paradise in her arms. Her mouth had a seductive curve to it that appeared to be whispering sweet invitations of lust as soft words seemed to float out of it like a vapour on the humid summer air. Ah, and her long, lithe legs seemed to go on and on as they were perfectly tapered and fit so seductively into her tight fitting jeans that she usually wore. Like Channa, she had an air of supreme confidence about her that seemed to say, "I am the master of my fate and the captain of my soul. Tread lightly men, because I am too hot to handle. Touch and you may get scorched."

Wayne, a frustrated poet, couldn't resist writing a song about her:

> *She is long and she is tall.*
> *When she walks down the street*
> *Her sway is hotter than a cannonball.*
> *She's the girl all men want to meet.*
>
> *Oh, that sway from left to right*

LYNTON WALKS ON WATER WHILE INGRID AND CHANNA DO AN IRISH JIG

Makes those jeans come alive.

How could she make them so tight?

This girl's got more buzz than a beehive.

She causes men's eyes to spark,

And like a flame ignite.

Those dangerous hips are likely

To start a brawl, a rambling fight.

She will always get her sweet way,

Because she makes men tingle when

She makes her hips sway.

Watch out. You're in the lion's den.

She sees through a man's game,

Because this woman doesn't play.

Lookout hearts, you'll be broken.

That's all there is to say.

When she walks past she is in the know,

Because she feels when to give and go.

So roll out the red carpet.

This doll's the star of the show.

J. WAYNE FRYE

LYNTON WALKS ON WATER WHILE INGRID AND CHANNA DO AN IRISH JIG

Now, contrasted to Channa and Ingrid, was the incredibly diminutive (5:2) and lovely Lynton, who, though a buzzing human dynamo that purred like a well-oiled engine, was an acclaimed accomplished athletes, a skilled dancer and talented singer. She was a bit more subdued with her sensually alluring charm. Her dark hair had been straight for years, but as a loving gift, her adoring boyfriend, Wayne, had given her a digital curl as a present which gave it great body and flare. It was as black as a raven and cascaded over her shoulders in great abundance, and it shimmered with a radiance that danced like the sun on a bright summer day. It was parted on the right side and a small shock of hair lay over her forehead and touched the tip of her left eyebrow as it floated to her left temple where it lay in glorious splendour.

Lynton's dark brown eyes were large and seemed to shine with a light from deep within that projected the purity of her heart. Yet, there was sensuousness in them that made the dark come alive as they shined a light that lured men to her like a moth is lured to a flame. They simply sparkled with delight. and when she batted them it was as if you could hear the flutter of an angel's wings.

LYNTON WALKS ON WATER WHILE INGRID AND CHANNA DO AN IRISH JIG

Many Asian women, because of mass media, which promotes the white culture as preferable, want to emulated western white females in skin colour and even go so far as to have nose jobs that lift and diminish the width of their flat Asian noses. Lynton was a natural Asian woman and proud of it. Her nose was flat and slightly broad, but it framed a dark, delicate, exotic face that was mostly free of makeup, as she needed no embellishments to her natural beauty.

Oh, but her most exciting, sensuous, captivating feature were her gorgeous, ripe, succulent, lusciously thick lips that seemed to be begging for a slippery, wet, scrumptious kiss from an adoring lover. They were the alluring illuminati of illusion laminating luscious illustrated letters of carnal excitement.

Now, her body was perfectly and magnificently formed in a 36-21-34 frame that was as taut as a bow in the hands of a skilled archer who was ready to let an arrow fly. Her legs were smooth and supple and she had calves that were muscular from years of playing volleyball and dancing on the stage.

LYNTON WALKS ON WATER WHILE INGRID AND CHANNA DO AN IRISH JIG

Finally, her greatest asset was a perfectly formed derriere that, according to Wayne, made her look as good going as she did coming. All things thoroughly considered, Lynton was simply a devastating explosive weapon of mass destruction. Now, as one might expect, Wayne saved his most luridly exciting and vivid song of epicurean passion for Lynton:

In the dark with her I came alive.
I found my way into the light.
Towards the wind I listen.
How her brown skin glistens.
She makes my limbs unfold.
This girl is worth her weight in gold.

Every moment every feeling is the same.
Seductively the night whispers her name.
How I long to rest my head on her breast.
In her arms I am blessed.
Watching her body in motion
Causes a sensuous commotion.

She has me on my knees,

J. WAYNE FRYE 40

LYNTON WALKS ON WATER WHILE
INGRID AND CHANNA DO AN IRISH JIG

And I don't care who sees.

My mouth mumbles words meant for her

With a touch of intimacy she won't fear.

Reading every sign her steamy body sends,

My love for her has no loose ends.

She makes my fire burn inside,

And my passion builds like high tide.

I dedicate my heart and lust.

I am the one she can trust.

Give me your sweet nectar of life

And end my hearts delicate strife.

In the refrain of an old song,

That just keeps me bopping along:

"If I told her she had a

Gloriously beautiful body

Would she hold it against me?

Would she hold it against me?"

Thus, these three extraordinary women were about to be drawn into a situation that would rattle the foundations of what many people believed, and would bring them within

LYNTON WALKS ON WATER WHILE
INGRID AND CHANNA DO AN IRISH JIG

the sphere of an evil man who was obsessed with getting his hands on the money that Ben Ramirez had stolen. And in the end, Lynton and her two friends would have to make a stand against evil.

LYNTON WALKS ON WATER WHILE INGRID AND CHANNA DO AN IRISH JIG

CHAPTER 2

TO GO INTO BATTLE AGAIN

Now there is a Hawthornian tale about a certain man who always hid his real self from view by wearing a veil over his face. However, sometimes the veil of deceit is not something physical, but is actually mere psychological deception that can be easily achieved in the hands of a master deceiver. It appears that the Reverend Augustus Haida, the new pastor in Taal, was just such a man. He wore not a veil, but his deception was much greater than anyone realized, and when he suddenly began to perform miracles, he would undergo great scrutiny by three young women who were healthy sceptics who never accepted anything at face value, but made sure that things were thoroughly investigated.

The Evangelical Church of God bell-ringer stood in the porch of the old grey church in Taal Heritage Town pulling busily at the bell-rope. The old people of the village came stooping along the street. Children, with bright faces, tripped merrily beside their parents, or mimicked their gait, in the conscious dignity of their Sunday clothes. This was a

LYNTON WALKS ON WATER WHILE INGRID AND CHANNA DO AN IRISH JIG

Catholic country, but the modern charismatic evangelical movement had not spared the Philippines from its incessant proselytising and spreading of what is often termed "old time religion." This quiet, out of-the way town had a very large contingent of fundamentalists, and the number was growing rapidly as missionaries pushing this particular kind of religion were furiously recruiting converts. Despite the often stark austerity of this type religion, the natural instincts could not be quelled, as dandy bachelors looked sidelong at the pretty maidens who were making their way the church, and fancied that the Sabbath sunshine made them prettier than on week days. When the throng had mostly streamed into the church entryway, the Reverend motioned them into the building. What was about to occur had been carefully planned and it was just part of a grand scheme, because no one knew much about Augustus Haida since he had only recently arrived by ship from the USA where he had studied Tagalog at seminary school so that the Filipino American could spread the gospel according to The Evangelical Church of God. However, the good Reverend was harbouring a deep, dark, murderous secret that had put him where he was, and he was about to practice a con game on an entire town.

LYNTON WALKS ON WATER WHILE
INGRID AND CHANNA DO AN IRISH JIG

How Augustus wound up where he was is a tale that will raise the hair on the neck of many as this was a man who oozed with evil, but as a masterful manipulator, he always came out on top. Well, except once that is – when he was put in jail for conning people with a stock scheme in the city of Silang. Yet, even that seemed to have worked out in his favour. In fact, being sentenced to three years, and serving 18 months was a blessing in disguise.

TheSilang prison was overflowing so he was shipped off, along with 50 other prisoners, to the prison in Palawan, where he had the good fortune to share a cell with Ben Ramirez. It was there that he constantly prodded him about the location of the money. Ben, aware of his intentions, was very careful to avoid any mention of the money. However, he did talk about his children and wife extensively, giving Robert Torres an opportunity to store up knowledge about the family that he would use to his advantage later on.

As Torres strolled into the church, he felt a certain smugness in what he had accomplished and was about to accomplish in a little town where he would work his manipulative magic. How he had gotten to this point was

LYNTON WALKS ON WATER WHILE
INGRID AND CHANNA DO AN IRISH JIG

the result of a series of circumstances that simply dumped opportunity in his lap.

Ben Ramirez had gotten very sick in prison, with a gastrointestinal problem that put him in the hospital, but the treatment received was, as one might expect, substandard for those that had been determined expendable by government that saw prisoners as unworthy of competent medical care. He was given some antibiotics by a nurse practitioner as the doctor had a golf date that afternoon and could not be bothered with a patient. The only problem was Ben was given a medication that acerbated the situation rather than helping it. It wound up causing his appendix to rupture and he died on the operating table.

Three months later, Torres was released from prison, and decided to journey to Taal and see what he might do about finding the money. Again, circumstances created for him a situation that would make it easy for him to arrive in Taal and become a vital part of the community.

On the ferry from Palawan to the mainland, he struck up a conversation with a minister who had been visiting the island to see if it really was paradise at it had been described to him back in the USA. He wanted to get in one last bit of excitement before settling down with his new job as minister for a Evangelical Church of God in Taal. It was the churches first and only outpost in the Philippines, and he was excited about serving his 280 parishioners. As he looked at Robert Torres, he was shocked at how much the two of them looked alike. When he commented on it, Robert said, "Yes, we look alike and think alike, too. You see, I am a lover of the lord, too. I have always wanted to be a minister, and bring his word to the people. I have studied the Bible for years and once did some sidewalk preaching in Manila. I was a great success at it, bringing in many donations that helped feed the poor and the homeless. It was one of my proudest moments."

"Ah, that is good to hear. Then you are a man of God. Perhaps you could come to Taal with me, and I can find you some work with the church," said the kind Augustus Haida.

"I am indeed a man of God. But tell me, does anyone in Taal know you?"

LYNTON WALKS ON WATER WHILE INGRID AND CHANNA DO AN IRISH JIG

"No, no I am a complete stranger in this land. I know no one here, and I have not met anyone since coming, except you," said the too trusting Augustus, as he thought he had found a genuine friend in Robert Torres. Now, that was Torres' stock and trade, making people think they had found a trusting, loyal friend in him. However, it was all a façade perpetrated by an incredibly skilled con man who had spent his life pulling the wool over people's eyes.

It was very dark that night as the two men stood by the railing, and Robert was observing that there were no other passengers out on the deck as the seas were rough and a storm was brewing. He smiled and replied to Augustus, "I don't think I want to work for you. Why don't I just become you?"

Augustus, bewildered and confused asked, "What?"

Smiling, the muscular Torres, quickly reached down, put his right hand between Augustus' legs, as he gripped his shoulder with his left hand. He picked him up and heaved him over the side of the ship, and the clamouring of thunder in the distance muffled his screams for help. As the boat plied forward in the dark waters, Torres smiled and whispered to himself, "Meet the Reverend Haida, the man who will perform miracles in Taal and also court a poor, mourning widow with two children and marry her. Damn, I am one lucky dude. The lord must be looking out for me. Now, I will use his name and collect money to benefit one of God's most deserving – me."

So, as Torres greeted people at church the first morning he arrived, the congregation was enthralled at his articulate manner and his kind nature. This was truly a man of God they all thought. Yes, Augustus Haida was special!

Now, Alana was a devout Christian who had left the Catholic Church in search of something more concrete to fill her life now that her husband had died in jail. She thought of the money he had left behind as evil, and wanted to return it to the bank, but Abby pleaded with her to do as her father had asked. Thus, the money was still safely sewn in Abby's doll, and she had the doll in her hand that morning as she and her mother were greeted by none other than Robert Torres, alias Reverend Augustus Haida. The plot was unfolding just as Torres wanted. He smiled at

LYNTON WALKS ON WATER WHILE INGRID AND CHANNA DO AN IRISH JIG

Alana, and touched the two children on the head, as he said, "What a lovely family, and where is the father of these two lovely children?"

Embarrassed, Alana bowed her head and told of her woe. The Reverend, with a look of deep compassion, said "Do not worry my dear. God will work things out. Remember that when one door closes another opens. I sense that other door is about to open for you."

When he gazed at Abby, she felt a cold chill coarse through her body. She did not like this man. He might be a man of God, but there was something wrong, very wrong about him. However, Louie took an instant liking to him as he was not as perceptive as Abby. In fact, Abby was the only one who saw through his skilled manipulative ways of ingratiating himself to people and conning them into believing he was filled with godliness and the love of his fellow man.

While all this was going on in Taal, Lynton, Ingrid and Channa were involved in an exciting adventure right across the street from Ingrid's house that was recounted in a

LYNTON WALKS ON WATER WHILE INGRID AND CHANNA DO AN IRISH JIG

previous book by Wayne Frye called *LYNTON BUYS A NEW CELL PHONE AND HEARS THE VOICE OF DOOM*. Right after that, the three women decided to take a nice vacation and rest up after battling demons of the foulest kind in a haunted house. However, their rest was short-lived, as they would face another evil. Yet, that evil would prepare them for a most hideous kind of loathsomeness, perpetrated by the vilest demon of all – man! Yes, the three young women were going to get in some practice before going up against the Reverend Augustus Haida. That battle against malevolent forces would prepare them to what was happening in Taal, and Lynton would remember the little girl named Abby who was from there and realize that she was threatened by calamitous wickedness.

This is not a story about supernatural heinous demons, but it must be brought to the reader's attention that these three women had experience battling supernatural forces with the aforementioned foray into pernicious villainy. This experience and the one that followed would put them in good stead to battle an accomplished con man like Torres (Augustus Haida) who would rely on people's superstitions and unquestioning faith to con them into believing that he was a man who could perform miracles. Relying on people's blind need to believe in something bigger than themselves had always worked well for Torres, because this was not his first foray into charlatanistic religion.

As Lynton, Channa and Ingrid enjoyed a vacation in the resort community of Taal, they soaked up the sun's rays on the pristine beach. These three women, as alluded to earlier, were all beautiful, and the God of body sculpting had worked overtime when he shaped them. The oldest of the three, Channa, had been in a relationship with a man for almost five years. Lynton had recently fallen in love with a writer from Canada who divided his time between there and the Philippines, but Ingrid was looking with intensity for that special man in her life.

Men, who are naturally and instinctively attracted to the physical attributes of women, were constantly introducing themselves to these ladies. Although flattered by the attention, Channa and Lynton were cordial but displayed no interest in the flirtatious actions of the men. However, Ingrid, although leery of men's motives in general, did take

LYNTON WALKS ON WATER WHILE
INGRID AND CHANNA DO AN IRISH JIG

particular interest in one young man who was visiting from the USA. He invited her to dinner that evening, and she cheerfully accepted.

Since all girls shared the same room, the young man, Bradley Cooper, very cordially asked if all three would join him for dinner. However, very discreetly, Ingrid shook her head indicating the answer from Channa and Lynton should be a very definite, "no thanks."

Bradley seemed a very nice and gentle man, and Ingrid was enjoying the evening with him as after dinner, he took her dancing at a local club that featured Karaoke, which is a favourite past-time for Filipinos. Ingrid was singing on stage, and she noticed that Bradley was having a heated discussion with another man at their table. The other man was Filipino, strikingly handsome in a sinister sort of way, had a crop of thick hair and appeared to be rather distinguished in looks with an air of authority.

As Ingrid finished her set, the man scurried away before she could get back to the table. There was no mention of the man by Bradley, and they ended the evening by having

J. WAYNE FRYE   53

LYNTON WALKS ON WATER WHILE INGRID AND CHANNA DO AN IRISH JIG

late night coffee. Bradley asked her out the next night and Ingrid gladly accepted.

The next day, Lynton and Channa kidded Ingrid about her new found friend, and Channa said, "I guess we will all be bride's maids soon."

Ingrid, who had been earnestly looking for that special man for a long time now, said "Well, I think it might be a bit early to get measured for your dresses, but he is very nice."

"So," Lynton interjected with a bit of levity, "I suppose you will not be sleeping in our room tonight?"

Mockingly, Ingrid replied, "It's a bit early for that, too, I think."

However, as they were soaking up the sun, Ingrid was thinking about the man who had showed up at Bradley's table while she was singing. Who was he, and why was he having such an animated conversation with Bradley? Ah, not to worry she thought, probably meaningless. Yet, she could not get the man out of her mind. There was something sinister looking about him.

The next evening, Ingrid went to dinner and the movie with Bradley. He asked her up to his room. She hesitated, but thought it would be delightful to melt in his arms and passionately kiss. She had wanted to kiss him the first time she say eyes on him, but he was too gentlemanly to make the first move. Ingrid thought "I'll make the first move."

Ingrid's romance with Bradley went really well, and as the week wore on, the girls settled in to the quiet village life of Taal Heritage Town. Of course, the girls were not avid church goers, but they did appreciate inclusive religion, as they saw it as a sometimes necessity. It was interesting when they met Ormond Assanti, an Indian businessman who owned the hotel where they were staying. He was, like most men, enamoured with the three beautiful women, and made it a point to run into them as often as possible. One evening, as they were having dinner, he asked if he might sit with them. The ladies, always gracious, said yes, and it was then that they learned why Ormond was always seemingly running into them. He was extremely tenuous as he said, "You know, I read about what happened in Laguna at that house. I can't say I believe it all, but I do believe that there are demons in this world, and I must say that you three women are the bravest people I know for doing what you did for that old couple."

Lynton, the one who had faced the most danger said, "Yes, we have actually been referred to as ghost busters since that book was written by Wayne Frye. I am afraid we are not nearly as brave as he made us out to be. Believe me, he did embellish things a great deal to make the book exciting."

"I was wondering," said the still timid Ormond, "if you ladies might be interested in something that occurred at our temple in the village south of here. It is a perplexing for me, and it grates on my psyche to think someone might be practicing deceit."

"Well," replied Ingrid, "we are eternally vigilant when it comes to deceptive people." So, go ahead, tell us."

Ormond began his tale: "Every year, pilgrims, Hindu,

LYNTON WALKS ON WATER WHILE INGRID AND CHANNA DO AN IRISH JIG

Muslim and Christian, flock to a temple south of here, as I mentioned. By mid-January, after 41 days of fasting and many kilometres of walking, pilgrims reach the temple in the middle of the forest and await a sign from God. They believe that it is a magical place."

Channa interjected, "Well, magic we believe in, but communicating with God is a bit out of our purview. He is a pretty busy fellow, so we try not to bother him with our problems."

Lynton and Ingrid vigorously nodded their heads in agreement as Ormond continued: "The temple complex has shops that sell CDs and DVDs of devotional songs, replicas of the temple and of course hand carved statutes from China, of all places, of Christian, Muslim and Hindu deities. The simple people who come there can ill-afford the exorbitant prices that are charged, but fork it over because they believe they are going to be blessed with good luck."

Lynton , shaking her head right to left, said "Religion is a corporation, just like any other. They are in business to make money so that the religious hierarchy can live lives of splendorous excess. I am sorry, go ahead with your story."

These are the Swami Ayappa pilgrims. And this temple, though not famous, is promoted discretely by the swami. The pilgrims walk barefoot and reach the shrine with bloody feet. After prayers, pilgrims wait on top of the hills, and at a pre-appointed time, a light appears on the horizon. The light blinks: one, two, three times and then goes out."

Lynton quizzically interjected, "You have seen the light?"

"I have seen the light, yes. It's like a flame. The moment this happens, everybody has this huge chant going up, Swami Ayappa, Swami Ayappa. It's like an eruption of worship. They keep saying this: 'Swami Ayappa, Swami Ayappa."

He took a deep breath and continued. "Jayakumar Barudi, head of the board that takes care of the temple and runs the festival, says it's like a spell. All these people stand there, just to see that light glow three times," he said.

LYNTON WALKS ON WATER WHILE INGRID AND CHANNA DO AN IRISH JIG

Channa asked in a very direct manner, "And what do the people believe then?"

"For years the light has been believed to be divine, the light of God. For all these years, pilgrims have come to the temple."

Lynton, without reservations at all, said, "It is fake. The shops, the swami, the board are all making money from it. True miracles, if there ever were any, are not performed for money. If this was truly a place of miracles, then the miracle of crushing greed would be the best one to perform by a God that truly is compassionate. This is a man-made miracle I am sure. My guess is someone is flashing the lights and the board and the swami under the guise that this is a divine phenomenon are making lots of money. That is the problem with religion. Remember when Jesus went into the temple and threw out the money changers? Things have not changed; religion was used to make money then and still is today. Why does the church expect a donation to light a candle? People have already put money in the collection plate to pay for the candles, but are expected to pay twice. That is greed, which Jesus preached against."

LYNTON WALKS ON WATER WHILE INGRID AND CHANNA DO AN IRISH JIG

"However, my guess is you could catch the lamp handlers red handed and expose them. Yet, there would still be those who believed. Some people want to be fooled. Logic and religion are not compatible. That is why faith is blind. You are not supposed to open your eyes and mind to question, because if you question, you might find out the truth. The pilgrims don't care who lights the lamps, when they go there, they are transported into the realm of the supernatural where demons and angels battle for people's souls. It does not matter how preposterous the whole thing is. They want to believe, and a charlatan knows that and plays upon it. Yes, we have been called demon fighters, and I admit to seeing things that I never believed possible, but I am still a healthy sceptic, because I believe only in the miracle I see personally, not the one I read about, and even the one I see must be proved beyond any reasonable doubt."

Lynton, now enjoying herself, continued, "A few years ago, in a Middle Eastern country, a 32-year-old woman, gave birth to a baby boy, who came out of her womb clutching a miniature Holy Qur'an in his right hand. Since that birth, the mother of the child, Kikelomo Ilori, has been receiving visitors wishing to catch a glimpse of the miracle baby and the tiny Qur'an. Local government officials, Imams, chiefs and Muslim clerics have all attested to the authenticity of the story. The tiny Qur'an was placed inside a transparent box and beside it, a basin where people drop money. Intermittently, shouts of 'Allah Akbar, Allah Akbar' are heard. The pregnancy was 11 months." Lynton smiled as she said, "I guess he couldn't read the whole Qur'an in only 9 months." They all laughed and she continued, "When the midwife delivered the baby, she noticed it was clutching something. You guessed it; a very tiny Qur'an was in his hand. Oddly enough, this midwife now lives with the baby's mother and probably sleeps next to the donations."

"The Qur'an conveniently was wrapped in nylon, making it difficult to flip through. Now, we know how Muslim women are treated, so, the explanation for the nylon wrapping was because it was a taboo for a woman's blood to touch the Qur'an. According to the Muslins scholars, God knows what he is doing."

Lynton took a deep breath and continued. "Well, to me, the answer is the cup the family put out for donations. That

LYNTON WALKS ON WATER WHILE
INGRID AND CHANNA DO AN IRISH JIG

is the one thing that precludes the miracle for me. Anytime money rears its ugly head, I am doubly suspicious."

"This brings up another thing. You know a lot of the people talk about Christians living by faith. Well, I totally understand and agree with that, but I also think that as you mature as a Christian or in any other religion, you live more and more by experience not by blind faith. The world is a pretty horrible place, and if people would embrace one another, rather than condemning each other, as religion often teaches, we could have heaven on earth now."

That was when Ormond got to the crux of his discourse with the ladies. "I am bringing all this up, because of something that has happened here. You see, we have a new minister at the Evangelic Church of God here in town. His name is Augustus Haida. There was a miracle rumoured to have occurred during his very first Sunday service.

Ormond was a highly intelligent man who obviously had great respect for these three women, and was bothered by something that he felt they might be able to help with because of their reputations for integrity and doing the right thing. Before relating his concerns for what was happening in the village, he posed a question: "If a myth precedes a fact, does that logically make the fact a myth?"

Lynton, the youngest of the three, and known also as the most stubborn, said "Well, I am pretty headstrong. It is something people point out to me, especially my boyfriend, but it has worked to my advantage often; although, I admit that it has also had the opposite effect on occasion. My point is that I am a woman who is determined, tenacious and even sometimes cantankerous when pursuing the truth. For example, let's take the infamous 9/11 attack on the USA by terrorists, although, I am of the opinion that what Wayne Frye once said about terrorists is often apropos in that one man's terrorist is often another man's freedom fighter. I do not think this applies in this case, because of the heinous nature of the act. Of course, the fact that the USA backed the illegal overthrow of a government in Chile on 9/11/1973 that killed even more people and enslaved an entire nation to a dictator for nearly 30 years is never mentioned. You see, it is the recipient of the terror that matters, and the USA is always given special dispensation. For example, if anyone else but Bush and Cheney had sanctioned torture of captives, the illegal invasion of a nation and the killing of hundreds of thousands innocent civilians, they would be in the dock for war crimes at The Hague. However, because of its power, Americans are never called to account for war crimes committed in its march toward enslavement of all humanity to corporate, unfettered capitalism, which they equate to democracy."

As was her custom when getting ready for a long discourse, Lynton took a deep breath and sighed. "On 9/11/2001, as we all know, two planes flew into the Twin Towers. I was doubly shocked when that occurred, because I had read *The Last Jihad* by Joel Rosenberg, and on the first page it puts readers into the cockpit of a hijacked jet, on a suicide mission into an American city, but it was written nine months before 9/11. I am also an avid fan of Tom Clancy, who wrote a book, Debt of Honour in 1996, about a Japanese 747 crashing into the Capitol in Washington, DC, killing most of the top officials in the U.S. government. Or what about the American television series *The Lone Gunman*? The first episode was about an attempt to crash an airliner into the World Trade Center. It was a government conspiracy to increase defence spending

LYNTON WALKS ON WATER WHILE
INGRID AND CHANNA DO AN IRISH JIG

by making it look like a terrorist attack. It aired in March 2001. Does that make 9/11 a myth?"

"We have been talking about religion and its use by so many as nothing more than money making schemes. There is great adherence by Christians to the story of the resurrection. Yet, large numbers of people say it is nothing but a myth, because there are many other tales of people arising from the grave and even ascending to heaven. However, the next time someone tells you that Jesus was a myth, and this is coming from a woman who is a sceptic, ask them to name one other resurrection story that stuck. Just one? I don't know of any and I have researched many examples of resurrection when I was in university. I think there is a reason why all the other stories have faded into the deep recesses of history to the point that you can't even Google the subject and get definitive search results listing all the examples. Jesus is a product, and is sold for profit."

Ormond was enthralled by Lynton's breadth of knowledge, but Channa and Ingrid just took a deep breath, as they were used to Lynton's philosophical discourses that would often keep them up late into the wee hours of the morning. They eased back in their chairs, sighed a bit and heaved out their generous chests in preparation for a journey into the realm of Lynton conjecture. It would be long, detailed and precise, and as always, very enlightening in the end, but getting there could be tedious.

Lynton leaned forward and looked into Ormond's eyes. "Science and faith are incompatible ways of thinking. They are separate realms. I'll tell you a little story. Back in the early 20th century there was a great deal of optimism in the mathematical profession that we were closing in on a theory to explain almost everything. What mathematicians were looking for was a set of constructions that made all of the propositions of mathematics form a nice, tidy, complete circle. Let me explain what I mean by this. In high school you study things like a triangle having three equal sides; therefore, it is an equilateral triangle. And then you do all these proofs and you work all this logic from it. Well, if you take that high school geometry book, there are always four or five things that the book starts with as premises that everybody knows are true but no mathematician has ever been able to prove are true. We know it's true because it works and it's all consistent, but it can't be proved."

LYNTON WALKS ON WATER WHILE INGRID AND CHANNA DO AN IRISH JIG

You could see the thrill in Lynton's eyes as she got great pleasure and satisfaction out of her intellectual forays into the philosophical. "In 1931 a guy named Kurt Gödel proved that it would never happen. And actually, I think that Gödel's Incompleteness Theorem is just as important as Einstein's Theory of Relativity. Most people have never heard of it, but let me explain what his Incompleteness Theorem says in as simple language as possible: Anything you can draw a circle around requires something on the outside to explain it, which you cannot prove. This applies to everything. It applies to a bicycle; if you build a bicycle, the fact that it's there relies on something outside of the bicycle. It's true of a geometry book, a software program, the English language, or the universe. Gödel's Theorem was a crushing blow to mathematicians as it meant mathematicians would make everything flow into a perfect circle.

Ormond's puzzled look motivated Lynton to go on: "the universe is like an MC Escher painting where you climb up the steps and all of a sudden you're at the bottom again. There's a book called *Gödel Escher Bach*, which takes Gödel's Theorem, Escher's paintings, and Bach's music and shows how they're all basically the same. For instance, in Bach's music, the notes escalate and they go up and up and somehow all of a sudden it starts with bass notes again and you didn't even notice. What does this have to do with my statement that science and faith are incompatible ways of thinking? Well, very simply, Gödel's Theorem says that you cannot do science without faith; it's impossible. You start with a fact that you know this because of this but you always go back to some fact that you can't prove. Now, what does science do? It says if you drop a cup from your hand onto the ground, it's going to fall every time. Only past experience shows that to be true. You cannot prove that it's going to fall again. You always have to rely on some assumption that you can't prove in science. One little extra thing I want to throw in here; the statement that science and faith are incompatible ways of thinking, separate ways of thinking that should be kept separate, is that a scientific statement? No, it's a philosophical statement. Even a statement about keeping science and philosophy separate requires philosophy. And the statement itself presumes that philosophy gets to say something about science. That's exactly what Gödel was talking about. My point is that religion is more times than not a philosophical impediment to human knowledge. Why, for example, are there religions that insist on going back to the Middle Ages or earlier as a sign of faith? Why is human progress seen as a detriment to faith? Why is it inappropriate to use stem cells to cure disease? Why is it improper to practice birth control? Why are same sex relationships verboten when the church tells us how important love is? Why must we endure finger-pointing and condemnation from an organization that is supposed to promulgate tenderness and affection?"

Although Ingrid and Channa sat quietly, one could see that this was old stuff to them, and frankly, a bit tedious. However, they understood that Lynton was trying to make a point as she continued. "The history of science is the story of one religious superstition after another being debunked by reason and logic. If you study the history of science, you'll find out that it got started in Greece and didn't go anywhere. It got started in Rome and it fizzled out and didn't go anywhere. It got started in ancient Egypt and in China – didn't really go anywhere there either. It got started in Islam, and every time in those places, it stalled. Why did it succeed in Europe after failing everywhere else? We all know it launched there and took off like a rocket.

LYNTON WALKS ON WATER WHILE INGRID AND CHANNA DO AN IRISH JIG

The answer is actually in the Bible. Well, in the Bible that the Catholics read and the Protestants don't that is, a through review of *Wisdom of Solomon 11:21* reads that *the Lord has ordered all things in weight and number and measure*. So, even the Bible says that all things are weighable, measurable and countable, that there is a systematic explanation for what goes on in the universe. So far as I know, no one else in the ancient world made a more definite statement about science than Solomon did in the Bible. Now, I have no proof Solomon really said that, other than the fact it appears in the Bible, so there, again, is a philosophical conundrum."

So enthralled was Ormond that he simply sat mesmerized as she continued. "Western Christianity believed that the universe was governed by fixed, discoverable laws, and that's what gave birth to science. The reason that science succeeded in the West and failed in all those other places was that in all those other places, there was no theological basis to believe this."

Ormond could not utter a word; only nod his head in agreement. Meanwhile, Channa and Ingrid rolled their eyes, because they had heard this discourse many times before.

Lynton was growing more intense with her words. "If you believe that it rained today because Zeus is having an argument with Mercury, how are you going to come up with a systematic explanation that doesn't invoke some kind of arbitrary, whimsical source? Christian theology believed that God could create the world in six days and rest on the seventh. While he was resting, his omnipotent power made the universe continue to do what he told it to do. Therefore, the great minds of the time actually viewed the study of science as a way of studying the mind of God."

Ormond, still mesmerized, managed a question. "And what of the accuracy of the Bible, the church says it is the divine word of God."

"The church, the synagogue, the mosque, the Hindu temple, the Buddhist monks profess a lot of things. Does that make them true? Whatever happened to independent thought? Why, in the USA, for example, are children forced to stand and say the pledge of allegiance every morning at school? Could it be that the government wants to indoctrinate future warriors to fight its wars? Why do churches insist on getting youths into Sunday school to study about Jesus? Could it be that they know you have to indoctrinate minds early, before they can form logic and coherent thought patterns that question things? If the church waited until they were adults, would they not be more likely to question and ponder? Why are children forced to memorize the Qur'an? Is it an attempt to instil at an early age, undying faith that will not question?"

"I have done extensive research and know that the Bible is a compilation of ancient stories told long before Jesus, before Moses, etc... Listen, there is no concrete proof that the Jews were ever in Egypt, and it is known that they did not, as slave labour, build the pyramids. St. Paul is venerated and many say he invented Christianity by making a rabbi named Jesus into God. Matthew, Mark, Luke and John were also venerated chroniclers of the Prince of Peace. Now, here is one for you. How many despots throughout history have been allied with the Prince of Peace in wars? George Bush regularly conversed with God. It was God told him to invade Iraq and free those people from tyranny and spread democracy. How convenient to have a Bible in your hand, while with the other hand you are pushing buttons to launch missiles to destroy innocent men, women and children."

"Paul Tibbetts was the pilot of the Enola Gay, which was the plane that dropped the bomb on Hiroshima in 1945. He was a religious man, but he had no problem dropping that bomb in what is the greatest terrorist act of all time on the atheistic non-white Japanese. So, is the Bible the divine word of God? Sure it is, if you want to believe it is. Hey, even Hitler believed in God and thought he was doing God's work by eliminating Jews, who most religions blame for the death of Christ."

"The short answer to your question then," Lynton said as Channa and Ingrid rolled their eyes and looked at one another as if saying to themselves, *yeah, it's about time for a short answer*, "is that accuracy is not the question those of faith are interested in. All they want is a miracle in their lives. In the Philippines, we have descended, since Marcos was deposed, into abject poverty, because the country was handed over to corporations at the behest of America which controls most of the world with its culture of greed. All most people have left now is the faith that one day in the sweet bye and bye their lives will be better. They all need a miracle, and religion offers them that. Religion has little relevance for the wealthy. It is reserved for those who have little hope in this life and need assurance that there is a better life waiting after all their suffering."

Ormond eased back in his chair, took a deep breath and said, "I am impressed. You Lynton are a woman of infinite wisdom."

Channa, ever perceptively sarcastic, said, "Oh no, now we will have to contend with Ms. Infinite Wisdom."

They all laughed, and Ingrid looked directly at Ormond and said, "So, what is it that makes you so concerned about this so-called miracle performed by the new minister?"

"Oh, it actually isn't just one, and the first one was more a sign than a miracle. Most say it was a sign of Reverend Augustus Haida being chosen by God. Then there is his courting of a widow who all in the village knows has a vast amount of money her husband stole stashed away somewhere. She has two children, and it appears that she and the Reverend Haida will probably be marrying."

Ingrid said, "And why do you think we can be of any help? We are not miracle busters. We are demon busters."

The three girls laughed uproariously, but were surprised when Ormond did not join in the laughter. Very seriously, he said "I am worried about so many people seemingly thinking this man is a miracle worker, a true man of God."

Lynton, equally serious, asked "What can we do?"

"You three are vanguards in the fight against evil. You, because of your exploits, have super hero status. I am concerned, because the little girl whose mother is enamoured with Reverend Haida, came in here one day to get something from the restaurant for her mother. As always, since she is such a precious child, I gave her some liquorice I keep in a jar by the front desk. I also gave her a piece for her brother and said, "Be sure and give it to him now. Remember, you must be a good girl and share.""

LYNTON WALKS ON WATER WHILE INGRID AND CHANNA DO AN IRISH JIG

Wiping his forehead, he continued. "She looked up at me and said the strangest thing. She said, 'Being good for me is natural. You know I am good, because I don't put up an act. Reverend Haida puts on an act with my mother and the congregation. I could never dishonour God by being one thing in public and another in private.' I was so shocked at what she said and the adult serious manner in which she said it. Abby is such an intelligent young girl."

Hearing the name struck Lynton like a bolt of lightning. Was this the Abby she had met at the mall?"

When Ormond described her, the physical description matched. It was then that Lynton looked at her two friends and said, "Get ready girls, we are about to go into battle again."

CHAPTER 3

MAKING ME A RICH MAN

Now, we know that Lynton recalled the meeting with Abby, and was concerned about her welfare. However, it is imperative that we go back in time a bit and see just what happened when Robert Torres, who became Reverend Augustus Haida, showed up for that first sermon at the church that he was going to use as a springboard to stealing that ill-gotten money from Alana Ramirez.

His first sermon was about a person who hid behind a veil. He thought it extremely appropriate to use, because it would make people think that it was not possible that the good Reverend Haida would use a sermon about deceit and then practice it. Ah, what a brilliant con man was Robert Torres.

The sermon: *One day a man wandered into a village and asked if there was a home for rent, as he wanted a quiet place to settle. The only problem was that this man wore a veil over his face. The fact that no one could see his face was troubling to the people in the community.*

LYNTON WALKS ON WATER WHILE INGRID AND CHANNA DO AN IRISH JIG

The cause of so much amazement may appear sufficiently slight. You see, this man, we will call him Mr. Smith, a gentlemanly person, of about thirty, though still a bachelor, always dressed with due neatness, as if a careful wife had ironed his clothes. But there was one thing most remarkable in his appearance. Swathed about his forehead, and hanging down over his face, so low as to be shaken by his breath, Mr. Smith had on a black veil. On a nearer view it seemed to consist of two folds of crape, which entirely concealed his features, except the mouth and chin, but probably did not intercept his sight, further than to give a darkened aspect to all living and inanimate things. With this gloomy shade before him, Mr. Smith walked onward, at a slow and quiet pace, stooping somewhat, and looking on the ground, as is customary with abstracted men, yet nodding kindly to those of his neighbourhood. But so wonder-struck were they that his greeting hardly met with a return.

Now, we all know that some women of the Muslin faith in this nation wear facial coverings for religious reasons, but this was a male, and one who apparently had no religious conviction, which also bothered the people, because I say

LYNTON WALKS ON WATER WHILE INGRID AND CHANNA DO AN IRISH JIG

to you, my new parishioners, that he who does not profess fealty to that great book, the Bible, is one who deserves to be suspect. The Bible is man's guide, and without it there can be no salvation, no home in heaven. We must all adhere to its admonitions or suffer the fiery pits of hell in eternity.

Now, people were so suspect of him that they began to whisper things about him being an escaped convict or a well-known celebrity trying to escape the limelight. There was a great meeting in the town hall one night and few could refrain from twisting their heads towards the door when a terrible racket was heard; many stood upright, and turned directly about; while several little boys clambered upon the seats, and came down again with a terrible racket. There was a general bustle, a rustling of the women's gowns and shuffling of the men's feet, greatly at variance with that hushed repose which should attend the entrance of Mr. Smith into the hall. But Mr. Smith appeared not to notice the perturbation of the people. He entered with an almost noiseless step, bent his head mildly to the people on each side, and bowed as he moved down the centre aisle. Mr. Smith had ascended the stage, and showed himself on

LYNTON WALKS ON WATER WHILE INGRID AND CHANNA DO AN IRISH JIG

it, face to face with the people in the hall, except for the black veil. That mysterious emblem was never once withdrawn. It shook with his measured breath, as he raised his palms and began to chant for the devil to abide with all there. There was a mass commotion as people frantically started to run from the hall. A wave of Mr. Smith's hand froze them in their tracks and the doors were bolted, unable to be opened.

Many people dropped to their knees and began to pray just as Mr. Smith said, "It is too late to pray now, because you have allowed me among you without lifting my veil. A sinister smile gleamed faintly from beneath the black veil, and flickered about his mouth, glimmering as he disappeared in a cloud of smoke. The doors were opened and the people breathed a sigh of relief.

"How strange," said a lady, "that a simple black veil, such as any woman might wear on a hat or that a Muslim woman might wear in deference to her religion, should become such a terrible thing on Mr. Smith's face! Something must surely be amiss with our intellects," observed her husband, the physician of the village. "But the

LYNTON WALKS ON WATER WHILE INGRID AND CHANNA DO AN IRISH JIG

strangest part of the affair is the effect of this vagary, even on a sober-minded man like myself. The black veil, though it covers his face, throws its influence over his whole person, and makes him ghostlike from head to foot. Do you not feel his evil?"

One week later, as all in the community avoided even looking upon Mr. Smith, there was a death of a man well-known to be a non-believer, but he was still revered by those in the community who were attracted to him because of his wealth. Consequently, many people came by his house to file past the casket and offer condolences to the family. The relatives and friends were assembled in the house, and the more distant acquaintances stood about the door, speaking of the good qualities of the deceased, when what they really meant was they coveted his wealth. Their talk was interrupted by the appearance of Mr. Smith in his black veil. It was now an appropriate emblem. The man stepped into the room where the corpse was laid, and bent over the coffin, to take a last farewell of the deceased. He whispered something into his ear. As he stooped, the veil hung straight down from his forehead, so that, if the dead man's eyelids had not been closed forever, he might have

J. WAYNE FRYE 81

LYNTON WALKS ON WATER WHILE INGRID AND CHANNA DO AN IRISH JIG

seen his face. A person who watched the interview between the dead and living, scrupled not to affirm, that, at the instant when the features were disclosed, the corpse had slightly shuddered, almost seeming to breathe again, though the countenance retained the composure of death From the coffin Mr. Smith passed into the chamber of the mourners, and thence to the door from which he entered. The people trembled as he reached for the door, opened it and walked out. Why they all asked did he talk to a deed man? Was he offering a welcome into hell that awaited the non-believer?"

One day there was a wedding and into the church walked Mr. Smith in his black veil. The first thing that people's eyes rested on was the same horrible black veil, which had added deeper gloom to all their lives and could portend nothing but evil to the wedding at hand. Such was its immediate effect on the guests that a cloud seemed to have rolled duskily from beneath the black crape, and dimmed the light of the church. The bridal pair stood up before the minister. But the bride's cold fingers quivered in the tremulous hand of the bridegroom, and the bridegroom's deathlike paleness caused a whisper that the non-believer

LYNTON WALKS ON WATER WHILE
INGRID AND CHANNA DO AN IRISH JIG

who had been buried a few days before was come from his grave to be married in a new body. After the ceremony, Mr. Smith joined the reception and raised a glass of wine to his lips, wishing happiness to the new-married couple in a strain of mild pleasantry that sent fright through all there. At that instant, catching a glimpse of his figure in the looking-glass, the black veil involved his own spirit in the horror with which it overwhelmed all others. His frame shuddered, his lips grew white, and he spit the un-tasted wine upon the carpet, and rushed forth into the darkness as a strange light descended from the ceiling of the reception hall in the church, seemingly frightening him.

The next day, the whole village talked of little else than Mr. Smith's black veil and how something from above had sent him scurrying from the church. That, and the mystery concealed behind the veil, supplied a topic for discussion between acquaintances meeting in the street, and good women gossiping at their open windows. It was the first item of news every morning and the last item of news at bedtime. The children babbled of it on their way to school. One imitative little boy covered his face with an old black handkerchief, thereby so affrighting his playmates that they panicked and ran from him screaming that Mr. Smith had found a disciple.

It was remarkable that none in the village dared lift the veil to gaze upon what was beneath it, but that is the way of the world. People are fearful of confronting evil. They wait for someone else to do it. Hitherto, whenever there appeared the slightest call for such interference, the good people had been guided by the good book that says evil must be confronted. Yet, though so well acquainted with this amiable weakness, no individual in the entire village, not even the ministers of the word, chose to confront this minion of evil.

There was the black veil swathed round Mr. Smith's forehead, and concealing every feature above his placid mouth, on which, at times, one could perceive the glimmering of a sinister smile. But that piece of crape, to their imagination, seemed to hang down before his heart, the symbol of a fearful secret between him and who? Were the veil but cast aside, they might speak freely of it, but not till then. Thus they sat a considerable time, speechless, confused, and shrinking uneasily from Mr. Smith's red, piercing eyes, which they felt to be fixed upon them with an invisible glance. Fear kept them all in check.

Now, one day, into this village came a man of unparalleled faith. Upon gazing at the man with the black veil, he showed no fear or trepidation. He, upon meeting with the townspeople, with calm energy and depth of character, refused to cow in fear at the sight of Mr. Smith. This was an affront to Mr. Smith, because he enjoyed instilling fear among the villagers.

This lack of fear by, oh, let's says Mr. Jones, began to make some of the other villagers ask if they, too, might grow in strength against this evil. Mr. Jones was a good example, who awakened a newfound faith in others, who decided to place their faith in Mr. Jones and his ability to confront evil.

From that time forward, no attempts were made to remove Mr. Smith's black veil, or, by a direct appeal, to discover the secret which it was supposed to hide. Mr. Smith could not walk the street with any peace of mind or with the self-assuredness that people feared him. The

LYNTON WALKS ON WATER WHILE INGRID AND CHANNA DO AN IRISH JIG

impertinence of the latter class compelled him to give up his customary walk at sunset to the burial ground; for when he leaned pensively over the gate, there would always be faces behind the gravestones, peeping at his black veil. A fable went the rounds that the stare of the dead people drove him thence. It grieved him, to the very depths of his tortured soul that people no longer feared him. Rather, he began to fear the people, because they were standing up to evil, refusing to bow humbly in fear. Their instinctive dread was no longer prevalent and it caused Mr. Smith to feel his own horror was interwoven with the threads of the black crape and now beginning to haunt him. In truth, his own antipathy to the veil was known to be so great, that he never willingly passed before a mirror, nor stooped to drink at a still fountain, lest, in its peaceful bosom, he should be affrighted by himself. This was what gave plausibility to the whispers, that Mr. Smith's conscience tortured him for some great crime too horrible to be entirely concealed, or otherwise than so obscurely intimated. Thus, from beneath the black veil, there rolled a cloud into the sunshine, an ambiguity of sin or sorrow, which enveloped the evil man, so that love or sympathy could never reach him. It was said that ghost and fiend consorted with him there. With self-shuddering and outward terrors, he walked continually in its shadow, groping darkly within his own soul, or gazing through a medium that saddened the whole world. Even the lawless wind, it was believed, respected his dreadful secret, and never blew aside the veil. But still Mr. Smith sinisterly smiled with ill-intent at the pale visages of the worldly throng as he passed by them. He loathed them for their faith, and his tortured soul wanted to wreck havoc on their lives.

Among all its bad influences, the black veil had the one desirable effect of making the villagers confront their fears and renew their faith, all because Mr. Jones had showed them how to live without fear. By the aid of Mr. Smith's mysterious emblem--for there was no other apparent cause, he became a man who suffered, as we all do for the agony of sin. Such were the terrors of the black veil that now had been turned on its user. In this manner Mr. Smith spent a long life, irreproachable in outward act, yet shrouded in dismal suspicions, unloved, a man apart from men, shunned by all. As years wore on he became a hermit, rarely venturing out. Yes, the good people of the village,

LYNTON WALKS ON WATER WHILE INGRID AND CHANNA DO AN IRISH JIG

thanks to Mr. Jones, were no longer living in fear and the evil had been stayed, totally arrested by the love this one individual was able to project. I say to you, always look for Mr. Jones, because he is among you and he will lead you to salvation."

The congregation all knew who Mr. Jones was. Yes, they had in the Reverend Haida, the real Mr. Jones. He had been sent by God to them to arrest their fears. The congregation leapt to their feet and spontaneous applause broke out. Robert Torres, the meek but assured Reverend Haida now as a result of murder, felt a warm glow inside as he realized his spellbinding oratory had captured their hearts. They were ripe for picking!

Robert Torres realized at that very moment that he had been preparing his whole life for the job he now had in this little community. Yes, he was destined to be a minister and use his manipulative abilities to fleece the flock and to capture the heart of Alana Ramirez and thereby get his hands on the one million pesos she had, no doubt, skilfully hidden. This was his destiny. This was his ticket to easy street.

LYNTON WALKS ON WATER WHILE INGRID AND CHANNA DO AN IRISH JIG

Torres was a strikingly handsome, and even as a youth he had used those magnificent good looks to his advantage. His mother dotted on him, because his alcoholic father never had time for her. And she was always telling him how handsome he was. That is when he would pretend shyness to get his way.

Robert had attended university where he was a stellar student. After graduation with honours, he attended law school, but in his second year he was kicked out for running nightly poker games in his room. No mind thought Robert, as he preferred the street con to the courtroom con. He simply moved on with his con games, doing so well at them that he always managed to be rolling in dough. His mother was dying from cancer, and so callous was he, that he could not cut short a con in order to be by her bedside when she died. Although he came close to being apprehended many times, he always managed to elude the law until the one time he was caught and landed in jail with Ben Ramirez as his cell-mate, but that actually worked in his favour, setting up what he felt would be his ultimate con.. He was not above felonious assault to protect himself from being caught, and his superb strength and skill as an amateur boxer kept him in good stead when fisticuffs were called for.

Torres was slim but muscular. At 6:0, he was an imposing figure and his body was as hard as iron and his skin was sleek as polished steel. He had a fastidiousness nature, a natural elegance in appearance, manners and speech. All the items of his wardrobe were flashy, but not in an awkward fashion. You felt that he would belong to any set in the world which he sufficiently admired. There was a romantic flare about him that made women swoon. He was as suave a man has had ever strode down a street. He had all the graces of privilege, and hid his working-class background with great ease. His thin face was resolute. You saw only its youthful freshness first, then behind the brightness a taut determination and his brown eyes seemed to dance with vigorous delight, but there was something hiding behind them, something deep within his soul that was a boiling cauldron of discontent.

His thick, broad shoulders seemed able to carry the heaviest of loads be they physical or psychological. He was a gladiator with words and never let an opponent get the best of him. With women he was so smooth they were soon begging for his amorous attention. So adapt at getting women was he that he looked upon them as chattel, mere objects to own for awhile, before moving on to someone else. They were just an easy con.

Robert Torres had great contempt for the church, but hid it well, because he knew that showing faith was a keen way to ingratiate yourself to people in a country where religion held great sway over everyone and even over the government. Robert's mother, drained by early widowhood and drudgery, finding her only emotion in hymns and the Bible, and weeping when he failed to study his Sunday school lesson had taught him from an early age to be fearful of God, but Robert was fearful of nothing – not even a God in which he did not believe. He loved going to church, but preferred the Protestant church, which he would attend after mass, because he enjoyed watching the ministers work their magic on the congregation, drawing people to accept God when they made the call, and how he got a thrill out of seeing the fundamentalists shout, lie on the floor and writhe in ecstasy when the holy spirit got hold of them.

LYNTON WALKS ON WATER WHILE INGRID AND CHANNA DO AN IRISH JIG

How he loved to be converted and sign pledges to give up, forever, the joys of profanity, alcohol, cards, dancing, and the theatre. The ink had hardly dried on the pledge when he was out doing all those things with great glee, and laughing about the silliness of having people actually write down there devotion to doing the right thing. What would the church do when they broke the pledge, take those who sinned to court?

Robert had spent almost every Sunday in church, not because of a commitment to God, but because of a commitment to learning the skills and techniques of those he called master marketers. Ministers were skilled at selling pie in the sky to those who longed for not just salvation, but for hope that there was something good waiting for those who had no hope on earth. Dangling golden laden eternity floating effortlessly in blissfulness on the clouds plucking a harp was a way to offer that hope to those who had no immediate prospects.

His favourite part of church was watching people who could ill-afford it plop money into the collection plate. Yeah, thought Robert, that collection plate was what he wanted to get his hands on, and he loved it when he heard one minister say to his congregation as the collection plate was being passed around the church, "Please Lord, do not let me hear the jingle of coins going into your collection plate, let me hear the soft rustle of paper bills that genuinely show the love of your humble servants." Yeah, paper meant at least 20 pesos at a time, as any thing less in Filipino money was coins. That was a minister, Robert thought, who would ride in a nice car, wear fine clothes and live in a fine home luxuriously appointed with material possessions provided by those who lived in squalor.

Of course, talking about the love of God was a great motivator, but teaching people to fear God was even better. Assure people that God was always creeping about to catch them in their secret thoughts and that God was counting how much you put in the collection plate. Sure, teach people how terribly dangerous it is to put off the hour of salvation and watch them cower in fear. He loved it when ministers utilized fear by warning people how unexpected things can end life – a train derailment, a Jeepney crash, a stroke or heart attack, a simple accident around the home. Keep those donations coming in to protect yourself just in in case. And then there was the devil to use as an adjunct to fearing the Lord. Hell was waiting for those who ignored God. Although, the nicest thing about God was he could forgive anything. All you had to do was supplicate yourself to His will, and of course, keep those donations rolling in to prove your love.

Robert first used his golden tongue for the Lord when he was visiting a town in the far north of Luzon Province and needed money to get back to school in Manila. He was absolutely broke, because he had been chasing women and gambling for three days. The woman chasing was highly successful, but his gambling ventures were not productive at all, and he found himself in dire straits with not even one peso in his pocket. What was his solution? He produced a paper cup he found on the street and started preaching on a busy corner. He even amazed himself at his ability. He began to pace up and down and his golden voice rang out like a nightingale chirping a sweet melody. "Come my friends. Come and hear the words of our Lord and Savoir. In the hustle and bustle of daily life I wonder how many of us stop to think that in all that is highest and best we are ruled not by even our most up-and-coming efforts but by love? Oh, how mighty love is - the divine love of which the great singer of charity, hope and eternal salvation teaches us in Proverbs? It is the rainbow that comes after the dark cloud. It is the morning star and it is also the evening star, those being, as you all so well know, the brightest stars in the heavens. It shines upon the cradle of the little one and when life has, alas, departed, to come no more, you find it still around the quiet tomb. What is it inspires all great men, be they preachers or patriots or great business men? What is it, my brethren, but love, sweet abiding love? Ah, it fills the world with melody, with such sacred melodies as we share the tender music of the love from our heavenly father."

"What are you permitted to hate by the great loving father? Hate the money changers; hate the bankers, who holds your mortgage and want you on the streets when you cannot pay. Hate the wanton scarlet women of the street, each of whom wears soft silk and in their bejeweled hands hold a ruby glass of perfidious wine to make you drunk with desire. Be you not drunk with wine or desire. They are both abominations that will doom your soul to the everlasting fires of hell where God propels all those who dare not follow the words he scribed in the most holy of all books."

As he railed against sin, in the crowd he noticed a fine looking woman of maybe 20 that titillated his libido. She was a bronzed-skinned beauty with a pink ribbon in her hair, pulling it back in a pony tail. He discreetly gazed upon her thirstily. His excitement at delivering a rousing sermon while dreaming of having her in his arms made the blood rage through his veins. Oh, how excited he was.

As the paper cup filled with donations, he could not resist winking at her. She coyly acknowledged his interest with piercing eyes that said, "I am available." Grabbing the cup and giving the people one last assurance that there was a special place by God's side waiting in heaven, he meandered off with the young woman, and went to the Hotel Sogo that specialized in two hour rentals. The seediness of the place actually heightened Robert's arousal as he enjoyed the grungy atmosphere.

Watching Robert work his magic with women was like watching a skilled illusionist who with slight of hand fooled an audience so well that they could not believe what they had seen. Robert was the master of deception.

His powerful oratory had not only procured him money to get back to school, but brought a lovely creature for him to enjoy before catching the train. Had Robert used his skills more appropriately, he would have been a master politician, maybe even President of the country someday. He would go on to other cons, unrelated to religion, but in the back of his mind, he always was saying to himself, "someday I will utilize my preaching skills to mesmerize and cajole people into making me a rich man."

LYNTON WALKS ON WATER WHILE INGRID AND CHANNA DO AN IRISH JIG

CHAPTER 4

SHE NEEDED LYNTON

Having Ormond describe Abby's looks assured Lynton that it was the same little girl she had met at the SM Mall in Dasmarinas. She had left a lasting impression on Lynton, because of her precociousness, intelligence and uncanny friendliness.

Lynton related the story of how she met little Abby to Ingrid and Channa. They all were curious as to why she had said, "Being good for me is natural. You know I am good, because I don't put on an act. Reverend Haida puts on an act with my mother and the congregation. I could never dishonour God by being one thing in public and another in private." Was there something deeply sinister going on in this little village?

These women had dealt with sinister elements before, and they had no fear, but they all knew that tackling what might be a cunning, devious, shrewd, manipulative charlatan of the cloth would not be easy. People, as a result of brainwashing propaganda by the church, thought of ministers and priests as something special. However, these three astute young ladies knew they were just ordinary men, who happened to have ministerial credentials. Those credentials did not make them holier than anyone else, nor did it mean they had a direct pipeline to God.

Channa was the first to speak out. "So, what do we do to nail this guy if we decide he is faking his sincerity of purpose? How do we explore his character, find out more about him and see if he is using smoke and mirrors to fool a lot of trusting people who just want to believe that there must be more to life than the daily grind to keep your head above water in a world where all the good things flow to those at the top of the economic ladder."

Lynton bowed her head, as in deep thought and then said "Right now we can do nothing, as we have engagements to fulfill at the Mall of Asia, Manila SM and the Greenbelt. We will give it some thought, finish our engagements and maybe come back here when we have the two week break. What do you say?"

Ingrid and Channa shouted in unison, "You're on girl."

LYNTON WALKS ON WATER WHILE INGRID AND CHANNA DO AN IRISH JIG

Before they left, the girls dropped by to visit Abby and her mother. The mother was shocked three well-known entertainers would have the time to visit them, and Abby was thrilled that Lynton had remembered her from that one day in the mall. She became instantly fascinated with Ingrid and Channa, but seemed particularly attracted to Lynton, because the two of them apparently had a special simpatico. However, as they were preparing to leave, Alana Ramirez dropped a bombshell on them. She looked at Abby, then over at Louie and said, "My children need a father. I am marrying the good Reverend Augustus Haida in two months. I hope you three will be able to make the wedding."

Shocked, the three cordially agreed to attend, but deep within they were wondering if they could conduct their investigation quickly enough to prevent the marriage just in case they turned up something nefarious in the Reverend's background.

While the girls were on their way back to Cavite, where Lynton lived, the topic of conversation was the Reverend Haida, and the detective work was about to begin.

LYNTON WALKS ON WATER WHILE INGRID AND CHANNA DO AN IRISH JIG

Ingrid was continuing her relationship with Bradley, who she found out had rented a place in Taal Heritage Village as he had decided to stay permanently. He promised to visit her at her home in Laguna. Lynton and Channa warned her against discussing their investigation of the Reverend with him for fear it might somehow get back to the townspeople. She cheerfully agreed, saying, "I am too busy with more important things than to discuss detective work with him." They all laughed, because they knew what she was hinting at, and the two girls were happy that their friend had found someone who seemed extremely nice.

Meanwhile, Reverend Augustus Haida sat in his lavishly furnished parlour, feet propped up, expensive hand knitted robe on, as he watched his favourite television show. He was reflecting back over all his cons as he was a man who found great satisfaction in knowing he had magnificently fleeced people all over the Philippine Islands and even once in Singapore. In fact, it was his Singapore fleece that led him to employ a confederate in his plans for the widow Alana Ramirez and the village of Taal Heritage Town. It was unintentional, but the old confederate had showed up unexpectedly in Taal. How discombobulating it seemed to

LYNTON WALKS ON WATER WHILE INGRID AND CHANNA DO AN IRISH JIG

Robert Torres, and he even considered killing him to make sure his identity was not revealed. Yet, the man had helped him fleece a widow out of 10,000 U.S. dollars in Singapore, so perhaps, thought Robert, he could be of valuable assistance in helping fleece the new widow and a few of the town's folks who were susceptible to religious manipulation. So, for 25% of the take, he joined forces with a man who was, with the exception of oratory skills, every bit as charming as Robert was, and equally nefarious, underhanded, manipulative and possessed the same ability to charm his way into people's hearts and minds.

Robert heard a slight tapping at his backdoor. It was his confederate who had also been in the same prison with him, come to ask about their planned miracle that was going to occur that Sunday in the church. They had come up with a sure-fire way to convince people that the Reverend Augustus Haida could perform miracles. Yes, that would make the donations come pouring in. They drank and talked about heir sexual conquests into the wee hours of the morning. Then, while it was still dark, Robert's confederate headed to the backdoor and slipped away into the darkness that was home to him and Robert.

LYNTON WALKS ON WATER WHILE INGRID AND CHANNA DO AN IRISH JIG

Magicians have been performing tricks for thousands of years that defied explanation. In ancient Egypt, long before Moses turned his staff into a snake, magicians had been performing that trick for the Pharaoh. Well, on Sunday morning, Robert, with the help of his confederate, was about to perform his first miracle in Taal Village. He was also going to announce his wedding date with the widow Alana Ramirez.

He sat down, poured himself a stiff shot of whiskey, which he kept hidden away in the cellar when not alone so that no one would know that he imbibed alcohol, because after all, he often preached that perdition was your destination if you succumbed to anything more than communion wine. Sighing, he thought to himself that he had not engaged in sexual relations for the three months he had been in Taal. His courting of Alana could not include sex until they were wedded, because she must believe him a true man of God who faithfully followed scripture. How he had wooed her gave him great satisfaction as he reflected back on his skilfulness. When he was introduced to her by one of the parishioners, he intentionally acted uninterested so as not to arouse suspicion, but gradually he

J. WAYNE FRYE 103

began to talk with her and he made it a point to accidentally bump into her downtown.

People had been forewarned in the Bible of false prophets that came in sheep's clothing, because inwardly they were demons looking for souls. Robert Torres was simply too slick an operator to be discovered by people immersed in old time religion who saw him only for what was on the surface. Alana Ramirez was a true believer, and extremely naive. What she saw was a man of character and the way he dotted on her children made her think it was time they had a father, and a man like Reverend Haida was perfect in every way. Still, for some reason, Abby did not like him. That bothered her, but she assumed with time, Abby would see the good in him and embrace him.

Abby had sensed the evil in Reverend Haida the first time she saw him outside church, as he stood under a streetlamp by the post office talking to one of his parishioners. He was a Filipino who had been born and reared in the USA, and she felt that he did not understand real Filipino culture. To her, he was as alien as if he had come from another planet. His skin was not as dark as most Filipinos. However, what bothered her most was his perfect Tagalog. He did not speak it like an American would; but rather, it was absolutely perfect with every little nuisance a native speaker would have. Why she asked herself was it so perfect? Also, despite the fact he had been brought up in America, why were his English skills so rudimentary?

That night by the lamp, Abby saw more shadow than man. It was as if the man did not exist. The man was hollow, and the dark shadow he cast was like a cloud of doom that seemed to ascend over everything in its path. When he looked her way and a slow smile crept across his lips it was like a slow recognition from him of her perception of his greed, his evil, his complete lack of any good. He knew she could see the real Robert Torres.

Still, Abby felt as if she was being unfair to her mom. Was it not natural for a woman who was young and widowed to long for a man, especially a man willing to become an instant father to her children? Could she be wrong about him? No thought Abby, I cannot countenance that man being my father. It was then that she remembered her oath to her father. Would her mother so fall under the spell of this evil man that she would tell? Surely she would not betray the promise to the man who stole for them.

Robert Torres knew that Abby was a roadblock in his pursuit of her mother and the money, but killing her would be too risky. He would try to win her over, but it would not matter in the end, because he would capture Alana's heart and with it, he would get his hands on the money. Still, he might not skip town, because he had found a gullible pack of sheep who would follow him into the fires of hell, so convinced were they of his goodness.

He invited Alana to his home a few weeks after that night, insisting that she bring the children, because he did not want people talking about them being there alone. The children were nervous, but seemed to settle into acceptance that there mother was now being courted by a man.

Alana Ramirez was a very good-looking woman of 32, who had kept her youthful figure and had large heaving breasts that were hard for Robert to keep his eyes off of. His whole torso swelled with longing. He threw back his arms, fists down by his side; chin up, like a statue in a park.

LYNTON WALKS ON WATER WHILE
INGRID AND CHANNA DO AN IRISH JIG

But when she edged so close to him that he could hear her breathing, he backed away, because as Abby and Louie lay on the floor keeping, he did not want to risk getting caught in a compromising position. Conjugal blissfulness would have to wait until after the wedding. So, he never kissed her except on the cheek. Ah, but a carnal fire was raging within him.

Robert drifted off to sleep, dreaming of what the wedding night would be like. Yes, he would enjoy pleasures of the flesh before he got his hands on that money, but the real pleasure he sought was the satisfaction of his lustful greed for money – money – money. Oh, how he loved money!

Ingrid, Channa and Lynton had little time for detective work, so they asked their friend Christine, who had a business in SM Manila Mall, to see if she might find out what she could about Haida as they rehearsed for their one week engagement at the mall. Now Christine, like them, was a woman of exceptional inner beauty whose kind heart had been recognized by Lynton's boyfriend Wayne, who had met her before he became enamoured with Lynton. When Wayne had visited Lynton for the first time, within a

LYNTON WALKS ON WATER WHILE INGRID AND CHANNA DO AN IRISH JIG

few days she had gotten on his Skype account, smiled at him while looking at the over 100 women he had listed and began to systematically, like a raging demon of devilry and mayhem, deleted each and every one of them. Wayne thought it was cute, but when she got to Christine, he pleaded with her, "No, no, please don't delete her. She is my very good friend. I am her Daddee Wayne. Please." Fortunately Lynton relented, and awhile later, she also became good friends with Christine, whose kind heart endeared her to Lynton as well.

Christine was a woman with many contacts and knew influential people who willingly looked for information on the Reverend Augustus Haida. What they found out was not what Lynton expected to hear. It appeared that he was a man of infinite kindness who had been born in Los Angeles, California and brought up in a Presbyterian orphanage. He went to seminary school, where he studied for the ministry, eventually fulfilling his ambition to go to his grandparents' native Philippines and bring the word of God to some isolated village there. There was absolutely nothing nefarious in his background. In fact, he was almost saintly.

LYNTON WALKS ON WATER WHILE INGRID AND CHANNA DO AN IRISH JIG

This puzzling information did not set well with Lynton, Ingrid and Channa who assumed that this man was a charlatan. They were convinced that the Reverend Augustus Haida was up to no good, not because of anything they saw, but because of their sense of abiding confidence in little Abby who saw something sinister about him. They would continue to investigate him, continue to look for that one element that might indicate something was amiss in his character.

While the three girls were in downtown Manila, Ingrid was visited by Bradley Cooper, who wowed her with his suave, debonair manner. So much so that she found herself in his hotel room in Makati City one evening. She was incredibly beautiful that night as always, and as she eased herself onto the sofa by the window that looked out at the bustling city, she reached up and let down her beautiful lustrous dark hair by removing her hair band. It fell over her shoulders and glistened in the light reflected from the neon signs outside their 14th floor window. She looked at him beseechingly and gave him the devilish little smile that set men's hearts to palpitating furiously as their libidos go into overdrive.

LYNTON WALKS ON WATER WHILE INGRID AND CHANNA DO AN IRISH JIG

Bradley put his right arm around her, pulled her to him and passionately kissed her, their tongues duelling with delight as they melted in each others arms. Ingrid, who had not been in a man's arms for a long time until she met Bradley, wilted with passion and romantic ardour. Was this, she thought, the man she had been waiting so long for?

They sat there in each others arms for what seemed like a millennium of time, not kissing, not fondling, just enjoying the rapturous delight of physical and psychological closeness.

As time passed, Ingrid could not resist asking him if he knew the Reverend Augustus Haida who lived in Taal Heritage Village. A troubled look came across his face, as he very tepidly replied, "No, I don't know him personally, but I, like everyone there, have heard of him. He is known as a kind, caring man who has, believe it or not, apparently been present when several miracles occurred. Why just last Sunday, in his church, something amazing happened."

Now Ingrid, unlike Lynton, was a devout believer, and was more open to religion than her two friends. However, that receptiveness to religion did not preclude her from having an inquiring mind. She had a healthy dose of scepticism, and what Bradley was about to tell her would pique her intellectual inquisitiveness appreciably.

Removing his arm from around her shoulder, Bradley took a deep breath and said, "I am only speaking with second hand knowledge, as I was not there, but apparently as he was giving a sermon, he turned, pointed to the crucifix on the wall and as he did, a tiny stream of blood poured out of the right side wound on the statue of Jesus. Obviously, everyone was amazed and enthralled. An examination of the statue showed the blood to be real. At the Reverend's insistence, it was sent off for analysis. He simply said, 'I have seen this before in other places where I have preached. I apologize for the attention this might draw. Believe me, I am just a meek servant of God, and I claim no supernatural powers. All I can claim, and that I do unapologetically, is love for my lord and savoir, Jesus Christ.' And with that utterance, he left the church."

The next day Ingrid shared what had happened with Channa and Lynton. Ingrid contacted Bradley to see how the blood analysis turned out and it was O-positive human blood that had seeped from the statue. Reverend Augustus Haida had insisted his blood be analyzed, and it was. It tested A-negative.

As the girls continued their performances, more profound things were happening in Taal. Now, one thing that causes people consternation is the Old Testament God's habit of desiring the reeking slaughter of every one who did not flatter him, which seemed rather anti-social and selfish, and makes one wonder whether all the wantonness in the *Song of Solomon* did really refer to the loyalty between Christ and the Church. Could *Solomon* just possibly refer to human beings being a bit horny? Hey, it happens. However, Reverend Augustus Haida was teaching in Taal that the vengeful God was still alive and well. You see, Robert Torres loved the vengeful God approach, because he felt fear was a great motivator. Robert was teaching his congregation that doubt was wicked, and that he was able to enjoy considerable ingenuity in exorcising evil from people, for a price of course. Only those who sacrificed their savings could stay the wrath of a vengeful God. It was recompense for sins. He insisted that there were no purple broidered ambiguities in religion. Every thing was either black or white, there was no in between.

With this vengeful God in mind, and with the previous miracle fresh in people's minds, Robert Torres, with the help of his confederate, was about to unleash another miracle on the good people of Taal. It, however, would be a vengeful act, because people needed to fear him as a representative of God. Instil fear in people and you gain great power. That was the theory used by America when it threatened nation after nation with military action. Well, it wound up breaking the USA financially and morally, but Robert was no student of history, and he recalled something he had once read when younger, a quote by Mao Tse-tung: "Power comes from the barrel of a gun." In other words, if you are not willing to use violence, then you will not achieve your goals. The government never hesitated using all kinds of violence against the people when they dared stand against the status-quo that kept them mired in poverty. The police and military were there, not to protect the poor from crime, but to protect the government, the wealthy and the powerful from the poor. It was their job to see that the poor knew their place and stayed in their place.

LYNTON WALKS ON WATER WHILE INGRID AND CHANNA DO AN IRISH JIG

Robert understood that violence was sometimes necessary for him to keep from being discovered in his cons. Robert was like the government, he had to protect himself at all costs, even if it meant resorting to violence. On this particular day, he, along with his confederate, had devised a plan almost as good as the blood that flowed from Jesus' wound on the statue. Robert's confederate had gone behind the wall where the statue was, drilled a tiny hole and on cue, he squeezed a tube that squirted blood he had procured from a blood bank in another province. However, this ruse was going to be even better. This would not just create awe. It would create fear, and fear was a great motivator. It was the way people were kept complacent and pliable.

It has often been said that the world is an illusion. Well, Robert Torres wasn't sure the world was an illusion, but he had studied magic and he knew how to create an illusion, and, to him, the world was very real, very cruel and only the strong survived, and he was strong. When someone told him the world was illusionary, he would say, "imagine the sound of bare knuckles knocking on a solid table: knock, knock, knock. It sure seems real to me! I believe what I can see and feel, and I see and feel plenty."

LYNTON WALKS ON WATER WHILE INGRID AND CHANNA DO AN IRISH JIG

Now, it is not the purpose of this book to underscore the philosophical elements of illusion, but it is important to understand that Robert Torres and his confederate were about to create an illusion to solidify Robert's standing as a man of God.

The real illusion here was Robert Torres or as he was now called, Augustus Haida. He was not what he appeared to be, and only little Abby appeared to see it. She had no idea what an illusion was, but as she stood by the lakeside on that Sunday morning with her mother and brother, she was about to get a lesson in the magic of the marketplace, the magic that captivated people and made them slaves to desires and fears.

An illusion is something that tricks us into believing a false idea. The dictionary says that an illusion is a misleading image, a mistaken idea. Yet, it seems that many people mistakenly think of an illusion as something that has no reality to it at all - something that does not even exist! Consider a stage magician. He's a master illusionist. Many people have seen the magic trick where he puts his assistant in a big box and cuts her in half with a saw. What we see is

LYNTON WALKS ON WATER WHILE INGRID AND CHANNA DO AN IRISH JIG

real. We see her head, arms and feet sticking out of the box. But we are not seeing the whole picture. We don't see that there is another person hiding in the box that makes up the other half of the assistant and creates the illusion of one person cut into two pieces. Even though our physical senses are doing their jobs perfectly, our incomplete picture tricks us into believing a false idea. Our false assumption that the feet that we see are the feet of the assistant leads to the incorrect conclusion that the assistant was cut in half. These two ideas are completely false but our raw perceptions are accurate. Once we see the bigger picture, we understand the true nature of the situation and are no longer tricked by the illusion. However, many people never see the bigger picture at all. What is that old saying, "They can't see the forest for the trees." They are not inquisitive or inquiring enough to explore the meanings behind things, or to simply ask why. These people accept things at face value, which is what Robert knew, and, for that reason, he believed that people of faith simply would believe an illusion, because they had turned their thinking over to him.

In a funny way, it can be said that an illusion is real. Yes, it has a reality to it. It's just that its true reality is different from what we first thought. We were tricked into believing a false idea. But there is something else about a good illusion that is very important and that is its persistence. Even if we know the secret to the magic trick, if it is performed well, it still gives us the impression that something supernatural just happened. Even though we are not tricked by the illusion in the deepest way, the false idea still resonates with people who desperately need to believe that there is some higher power, something that is controlling their lives, because most people cannot control their own lives, because outside forces are always dragging them into despair through manipulation or force.

Consider the moving images that you see on the big screen at the movies. Surprise! There aren't any moving images! Not one! Even though the art form is called "the moving pictures," you have never seen a single moving picture. It is just a series of still pictures being projected on a film that is threaded though a projector. The same is true for TV. Instead of true motion, we observe many still pictures presented to us one at a time so rapidly that our minds interpret all those still images as a moving image. And again, even when we know the truth, the illusion still

LYNTON WALKS ON WATER WHILE INGRID AND CHANNA DO AN IRISH JIG

persists. The false idea still appears as if it is true. You always observe what appears to be smooth motion even though there isn't any motion at all.

Now, Robert Torres knew all this, because he was an incredibly intelligent man, who, had he wanted, could have applied his intelligence to legal things and been very successful in life. He was fascinated with the sun travelling across the sky. You see, he knew that was an illusion, because the sun did not travel across the sky, rather the earth rotated on its axis and thereby created an illusion of the sun moving.

Robert, as he stood there among the throng of people, almost laughed at how easy it was to fool people and get them to believe whatever you told them to believe, so desperate were they for hope in their lives.

Now, an intelligent person might point out that the sun does indeed move through space. The sun and the entire solar system are orbiting around the center of the galaxy and one orbit takes about 250 million years. But the apparent motion of the sun traveling across the sky is due entirely to the spinning of the earth, not the motion of the sun traveling through space. Of course, Robert thought, how many people know this, and even if they knew, they were still gullible enough to put their faith in a man who was a charlatan.

People had once believed the claim that they would be flung off the surface of the spinning earth, and that birds would have to fly hundreds of kilometres an hour just to stay above one spot. People know things, but willingly accept that in which they really don't believe because they are fearful. Yes, there is that word fearful again. Many people today believe that Copernicus waited until the end of his life to publish his ideas because he did not want the ridicule of his peers and the condemnation of the Church. Yes, the church has historically stood in the way of human progress, because it saw that progress as a threat to its power. Fortunately, today the church does not play a dominant role in matters of science and astronomy; that role is now handled by the scientific community. Yet, getting on the "wrong" side of that force can still be a disaster for people, even if one's viewpoint is worthy of proper consideration and more investigation. In many states

LYNTON WALKS ON WATER WHILE
INGRID AND CHANNA DO AN IRISH JIG

in America, there is a steady march backward as laws demanding the teaching of creationism are being passed to counter the teaching of evolution. Many textbooks must state that evolution is an unproven theory. These are the same people who demean and ridicule the Muslin world for being bound so rigidly to the Qur'an, but they have no problem forcing regimented dogma onto impressionable school children.

The power of ridicule continues to be very strong even though it is virtually overlooked as a force that shapes the beliefs of a society and therefore the beliefs of most individuals in that society. Muslim, Christian, Jew, Hindu, Buddhist, etc. does not matter, when science and religion clash, the uninformed, the un-inquiring stand with the church against scientific fact.

With this knowledge, Robert Torres looked out at his enthralled, captivated congregation that thought they had gathered to witness a simple baptism of a child, but as Robert finished the baptism, he looked out among the people and said, "God is good, but when it is called for, he can rain down his wrath."

LYNTON WALKS ON WATER WHILE INGRID AND CHANNA DO AN IRISH JIG

Little Abby, though young, had never particularly cottoned to the idea that you were suppose to fear God. Her father had once told her, "darling, fear many things – fear the government because it is corrupt, fear the bank because it has no heart, fear the policeman because he works for those who want to keep you down, fear the weather because it can be harsh, fear the church because it can be intolerant, but do not fear the God manufactured by man to control you. That is not God. That is a vassal of man to make sure you are cloaked in darkness and kept from thinking for yourself.

The others there that day trembled in fear at what occurred, but not Abby; she stood stoically as Augustus Haida raised his hands and pointed at the sun and said, "I tell you that the wrath of God is real. I tell you that he is appalled by what he sees."

The imagination is the crystalline lens of our minds. It refracts the luminous rays of our thoughts and magnifies the images of all our perceptions. The scope of our vision is so small that to see rightly in this narrow world we must see things larger than in nature. Robert Torres had studied a

J. WAYNE FRYE

book on Houdini's magic, and he knew, like Hitler, that the bigger the lie, the more likely people were to believe it. What he did that day was a big lie, and people there, with the exception of Abby, believed what they saw, when in fact, what they saw was an illusion perpetrated by a master of deception.

Now, Robert had studied the sun and its position each day for a week, and he knew exactly where it was at a given time. Having studied the miracle at Fatima, he was about to unleash his own Fatima.

Perhaps a bit of explanation would be good for those readers not familiar with the so-called Miracle of Fatima or Miracle of the Sun since it was the catalyst for the miracle that Robert performed that day.

The Miracle of the Sun (Portuguese: *O Milagre do Sol*) was an event which occurred on 13 October 1917, attended by 30,000 to 100,000 people gathered near Fátima, Portugal. Several newspaper reporters were in attendance and they took testimony from many people who claimed to have witnessed extraordinary solar activity.

LYNTON WALKS ON WATER WHILE INGRID AND CHANNA DO AN IRISH JIG

According to these reports, the event lasted approximately ten minutes. Three children (Lucia dos Santos, Jacinta Marto and Francisco Marto) who originally claimed to have seen Our Lady of Fátima, also reported seeing a panorama of visions, including those of Jesus, Our Lady of Sorrows, Our Lady of Mt. Carmel, and of Saint Joseph blessing the people. The event was officially accepted as a miracle by the Catholic Church in 1930. Of course, this is the same church that now fast-tracks sainthood for all the popes. For some reason, modern day popes are more worthy of sainthood than those from the past, but in an era when pop-icons are entering the status of billionaires and people worship them like Gods, why shouldn't popes also be afforded pop star status? Are people's lives so mundane that the news shows are now headlined with what media whores like the Khardashians are doing? People dying of feminine, wars breaking out all across the world are only minor irritants when compared to what is going on with the privileged classes. What the royal leeches of England are having for breakfast or what they are wearing is much more important than feminine in Africa that is killing millions or the work of genuinely devoted people to eradicate poverty in the world. Modern

LYNTON WALKS ON WATER WHILE
INGRID AND CHANNA DO AN IRISH JIG

media has made a mockery out of genuine news, and Robert Torres was about to join in the mockery.

Robert was aware of how people in the small Portuguese village were captivated by the Miracle at Fatima, where three young shepherd children had predicted that at high noon the "lady" who had appeared to them several times would perform a great miracle in a field near Fátima called Cova da Iria. According to many witnesses, after a period of rain, the dark clouds broke and "the sun" appeared as an opaque, spinning disc in the sky. It was said to be significantly duller than normal, and to cast multicoloured lights across the landscape, the shadows on the landscape, the people, and the surrounding clouds. The sun was then reported to have careened towards the earth in a zigzag pattern, frightening those who thought it a sign of the end of the world.

The event was attributed by believers to Our Lady of Fátima, a reported apparition of the Blessed Virgin Mary to the children who had made predictions of the event. The children stated that the Lady had promised them that she would on 13 October reveal her identity to them and provide a miracle so that all may believe. Many scientific analyses since have explained what happened, but people of faith are not interested in scientific explanations, and Robert knew that. People with no hope need to believe in miracles.

Well, Robert Torres, or as he was now called, the Reverend Haida, knew how to perform miracles, as he had once worked an elaborate scam with a magician. It was not really all that complicated, but it took great timing and coordination. Robert and his confederate, the night before, had trekked up the side of Taal Volcano with a giant mirror. They placed it on the side facing where the sun appeared on the horizon every morning and put a black cloth over it. A study of geomantic reflection properties let Robert figure out that if properly placed; the mirror would refract the sun's image onto the shore line and make it appear to dance about in the sky. The two men synchronized their watches and decided that right after the baptism at 8:05 the black cloth would be pulled from the mirror and the angle it was placed at would make the sun appear to dance in the sky as Robert made sure people's focus would be on the ground.

LYNTON WALKS ON WATER WHILE INGRID AND CHANNA DO AN IRISH JIG

As Robert said, "God is good, but when it is called for, he can rain down his wrath," he pointed toward the ground by the shoreline and continued. "Today is a day of celebration, but never confuse happiness with contriteness. We must all be willing to humble ourselves before a God who can be vengeful if called upon to be so."

Exactly at that time, the cloth was pulled from the mirror, and the sun's reflection began to dance upon the ground, spin and circle as the confederate wiggled the mirror. Suddenly it stopped as Robert's confederate placed the cloth over the mirror 30 seconds later.

Robert could feel cold chills run up and down his spine as the congregation shouted, "miracle, miracle, miracle!" Yes thought Robert, a miracle created by your miracle making minister. However, in the crowd was one person who scoffed at the so-called miracle. While Alana Ramirez was filled with love and admiration for this great man of God, little Abby stood in completive thought. She had once been told by her father, "Abby, do not always believe what you read or what you see. It is easy to fool fools. The world is full of people who accept everything at face value. If someone tells you to do something, always ask why. Never accept anything without question. That includes your minister. He is only flesh and blood, and is no closer to God than you are. Just because he wears a clerical collar – that does not make him any holier than you are. You don't need a minister to find God, you don't need a church to find God, and you don't need to pray to find God. God is inside you, and he is always there."

There are those among us who have the skill to pull the wool over our eyes, and make us believe the unbelievable. It is almost imperative that mankind believe in miracles, because with almost half the world mired in abject poverty, a miracle is the only way out for most people. Even for the middle class, most of whom are only a pay check or two away from slipping into poverty, a miracle is their only hope. In a world where corporations own the homes we live in through mortgages or rental agreements, where corporations control the government, where corporations control the food we eat, where corporations now even own the water that flows through our taps, the only real hope is a miracle. Unfortunately, there appears to never be any economic miracle for the used and abused.

LYNTON WALKS ON WATER WHILE INGRID AND CHANNA DO AN IRISH JIG

That day, Abby was the only one who saw through the smoke and mirrors. Abby looked at Reverend Haida and repulsion overwhelmed her. Yes, this man was repulsive, and she knew this was no miracle, and that the people around her were fools for believing a magician's trick. She needed help. She needed Lynton.

LYNTON WALKS ON WATER WHILE INGRID AND CHANNA DO AN IRISH JIG

CHAPTER 5

UNIMAGINABLE BURDENS OF DESPAIR

"Being good for me is natural.
You know I am good,
because I don't put up an act.
Reverend Haida puts on an act
with my mother and the congregation.
I could never dishonour God
by being one thing in public
and another in private."

A man died, when he realized it, he saw God moving toward him with a suitcase in his hand. God looked at him forlornly and said, "Alright son, it is time to go."

The man, a bit puzzled, said, "Now? So soon? I had a lot of plans."

Again, God said, "I'm sorry, it is time to go."

Determined to stay, the man decided to ask God a question: "What's in the suitcase, God?"

LYNTON WALKS ON WATER WHILE INGRID AND CHANNA DO AN IRISH JIG

God answered, "Your belongings."

Confused, the man said, "You mean my clothes, my money?"

God replied, "Those things were not yours. They were only transitory items accumulated by you."

The man asked, "Is it my soul?"

God replied, "You never had a soul. You were empty inside."

The man reached out for the suitcase and God handed it to him. The man opened it and it was empty. The man realized that his whole life had been lived for himself, not for anyone else. He was empty inside.

This emptiness inside described Robert Torres. He was devoid of a soul, so callous was he that even murder to achieve his aims was acceptable. The murder of the Reverend Augustus Haida had never crossed his mind once he had tossed him into the ocean.

LYNTON WALKS ON WATER WHILE INGRID AND CHANNA DO AN IRISH JIG

Behold, the greatest magician is the mind! It is that which makes the memory yield its fruit, which realises beforehand the possible, and invents even the impossible. To the mind, miracles cost nothing. The mind can transport houses and mountains through the air, place whales in the sky, a star in the sea, give a paradise of belief, offer kingdoms to commoners and make the heart rejoice in that which is an illusion. Robert Torres knew that the imagination made it possible for him to deceive; it allowed him to embroider fables and symbols on the veils of the great mysteries that people wanted answered. He told stories to the children, and spun legends for the adults. He could make the thundering Gods and exterminating angels appear on the hills, and the virgins long to formicate with him. He made predictions and bent facts to accommodate those predictions. He was making himself the nurse of hope and the accomplice of despair. He made himself the gilded saint but inside he was the burned out cinder of the devil. He healed with illusion and killed with falsities. He created enthusiasm and belief, almost beyond the outer limits of the possible with his empire of falsehoods. He created a belief in happiness and gave it with illusionary skill, for so long as he could keep the people fooled.

LYNTON WALKS ON WATER WHILE INGRID AND CHANNA DO AN IRISH JIG

The imagination is the crystalline lens of the mind. It refracts the luminous rays of our thoughts and magnifies the images of all our perceptions. The scope of our vision is so small that to see rightly in this narrow world we must see things larger than in nature. People, devoid of hope and easy prey to manipulators like Robert Torres, never accomplish anything great, for everything appears to them in mean proportions. The astronomer contemplates the universe and imagines the Infinite; the believer contemplates nature and imagines God. In truth, the imagination is greater than thought. Science is trumped by faith, because people want to believe the unbelievable, because they have no hope in a world based on the lies of the powerful, the corporations, and the governments that enslave.

Collective imaginations achieve the results of the desired by manipulative entities like Robert Torres who know people are willing to let others do their thinking for them. Heroes grow greater, not because they are great, but because those who worship them are weak. The privileged classes, the celebrities, the powerful are raised upon superb pedestals and adored, because the adorers have nothing but emptiness in search of meaning to lives that are utterly meaningless. Life is life, why does it have to have meaning? It is; therefore, it is. It is. It is.

Torres was only a raging screaming tribune of banality, but, in his own way, a man of genius, that is to say a despot of the human imagination. It is because the poetry of people loves splendid crimes and meaningless virtues, because the mask of the magician is a grimace that would raise laughter but deep within it evokes horror, whilst the medal of each person's soul is actually a majesty which imposes itself on the worship of that which cannot in its depth offer any hope, but on the surface seems to offer promise.

Little Abby Ramirez knew the depravity of soul that was represented by Augustus Haida and saw within it an evil that had captured her mother in its grasp. That day at the lakeshore, the reverend announced his engagement to Alana Torres, and Abby knew that even her mother had fallen prey to the evil he represented, and she saw her poor brother being scooped up in the same evil. Yes, Louie was going to tell where the money was hidden, if Alana Torres did not. For that reason, little Abby set out for the SM Mall in Manila that was almost 3 hours away. Yes, she would risk all to find that lady who shined a beacon, a light of love on her that day in Dasmarinas. She walked away from the throng of people congratulating her mom and the Reverend Haida. She needed hope, and that hope was only available from Lynton Viñas, the beacon of light that shined so brightly in the mind of a little girl who carried unimaginable burdens of despair upon her shoulders.

CHAPTER 6
SOMETHING SINISTER ABOUT THIS MAN

Searching for something that may never be known,

She has confronted he who has a heart of stone.

Memories of what once was flicker in her head.

Now, she faces each lonely day with dread.

Others cannot see what is hidden from sight.

Ah, that man with her mother causes fright.

A ray of sunshine leads her away.

In her warm embrace she begs to lay.

Deception has caused her faith to stray,

simple gestures are life's way to say

Release the burden as it cannot stay.

Crumble your thoughts and throw them away.

Discover strength to start a new page.

No longer alone, slip from the cage.

Bruised and broken you now can see

she who will help set you free.

If misery finds one point of real hope, it is by pulling the lever of love. Abby had sensed that love, that kindness, that caring in Lynton. That is why she was going to Manila.

LYNTON WALKS ON WATER WHILE INGRID AND CHANNA DO AN IRISH JIG

When one knows and when one wills, one ought to have the courage to dare. This was little Abby Torres, who, like Lynton when she was young, refused to take things at face value. Lynton had dreams, but she also had nightmares. Lynton had endured great hardship, probably much worse than Abby, but she never gave into adversity. Fortunately, it was during a nightmarish stage when she met Ingrid, who like a rock, stood by her through adversity and let her know someone cared. That was why their friendship had endured. Adversity makes the best friends. That is when you know the true meaning of friendship. It is easy to be a friend when things are going well, but the true mark of a friend is someone who stands by you when all others forsake you.

Lynton was an architect of hope for many in her family and for a large cadre of friends. To all who knew her, she was a towering cathedral of strength and endurance. She had the placidity of a saint but the fortitude of a warrior. She understood the enigma of good and evil; she understood the dark shadows that blotted out hope for so many. She knew that the real miracles of life occurred when you overcame the darkness with the true beauty of a golden light that shines within.

LYNTON WALKS ON WATER WHILE INGRID AND CHANNA DO AN IRISH JIG

A little bit of love, in a world where it is in short supply, is what works real miracles. A small act of love can shake entire populations, arrest despair, cause the walls of hopelessness to crumble and heal the sick of heart. It amplifies wisdom, defeats folly, sanctifies truth, and glorifies acceptance and understanding. And those were the elements that defined Lynton Viñas.

The Robert Torres' of the world owe most of their successes to their power to manipulate and blind people to the truth. He was not a minister of the church. He was a minister of mayhem. These are the people who forbid others to partake of the forbidden fruit, while they sit at the table of hypocrisy and ravenously devour it. This was the hypocrisy represented by Robert Torres.

Love sows the seed from which is destined to develop the harvest of life. People like Lynton are the Pegasus of the hope, while individuals like Robert Torres are the Hippogriff of the Paladins. Within Lynton is a latent light that manifests itself by a sort of internal phosphorescence. It is this which illumines and colours the phantoms of our visions and our dreams, and exhibits to people like Abby an extreme goodness that is a beacon that shines like a laser into the hearts of all who bask in the light.

Abby had no money, so her method of getting to Manila was a bit unconventional. She waited for a truck, any truck to come by and come to a halt at the only stop light in town. Fortunately, one came by with a load of chickens. She simply hoped up on the truck bed, wedged herself in between some cages and rode all the way to Makati, where she managed to convince a Jeepney driver that her mother was waiting for her at SM Manila, and she had no money to get there, so she was putting herself in his kind hands. Those sad brown eyes touched his heart and he drove Abby to the mall for free, letting her sit up front with him. She thanked him and went inside, looking for Lynton, whom she had found out through checking with the SM Malls web site in an intern café, where she managed a free hour on the internet, was appearing for one week. Abby knew that her mother would be worried and was probably scurrying through the entire village looking for her, but with no money, she was unable to call. However, she knew she could get Lynton to call. It was 1:30 and the show started at 2.

LYNTON WALKS ON WATER WHILE INGRID AND CHANNA DO AN IRISH JIG

Now, it is well-known through the Philippines that the best mall show is put on by *THE SINGING AND DANCING THREE* troupe. As Lynton went on stage to sing her introductory tune while Ingrid and Channa danced poetic representations of sadness behind her, Lynton performed with perfection the song and music that Wayne had introduced her to a few months before. It was a powerful song expressing sadness, humility and regret. In fact, it had been voted, by music critics, the saddest song ever written, and Lynton's powerful emotional rendition brought tears to people's eyes as they could feel the pain and agony in every word she modulated with deep emotion. For Lynton, singing a sad song was a way of letting the audience know that she shared the collective pain that all humanity has. Whether it was a lack of money to put food on the table, living under oppression, the death of a loved one or the loss of the love of your life, the pain was real and Lynton knew each individual wanted to know someone cared. In a world where government turned a blind eye to the pain and suffering of its citizens, where economic injustice was not a concern, where pain and suffering as a result of that injustice was sanctified and accepted by the church, in Lynton Viñas there was a deep, abiding voice of reason and a plea for compassion. The song she sang, Hank Williams' *I'm So Lonesome I Could Cry*, had true relevance that day for little Abby Torres, as she stood by the railing on the second floor looking down at the amphitheatre on the first floor, listening to every word, tears flowing down her eyes as she realized that her daddy was gone forever, and that the only person she felt she could rely on was Lynton. Thought the song was about a lost sweetheart, in Abby's young mind, it was about losing her champion, the man whom she always relied on – her daddy.

Hear that lonesome whippoorwill
He sounds too blue to fly
The midnight train is whining low
I'm so lonesome I could cry

I've never seen a night so long
When time goes crawling by
The moon just went behind the clouds
To hide its face and cry

Did you ever see a robin weep

LYNTON WALKS ON WATER WHILE INGRID AND CHANNA DO AN IRISH JIG

When leaves begin to die?
Like me, he's lost the will to live
I'm so lonesome I could cry

The silence of a falling star
Lights up a purple sky
And as I wonder where you are
I'm so lonesome I could cry

There are times in every individual's life when a hidden hand of demonstrable fate seems to benevolently reach down with assuredness and touch our shoulders. That day, as the three young women were completing their last performance before taking a week's break, that hand of fate was placed upon Lynton's shoulder. It was a warm hand of circumstance that said to her, "here is a girl who has nobody but you to help her. Reach out and lift her up from the pit of despair."

Fate can be a lonely hunter, but on this day, Lynton, for some unknown reason, glanced up at the second floor and her eyes locked on little Abby. Lynton knew instantly that there was something dreadfully wrong and that there was no such thing as accident. It was simply fate misnamed and she and Abby were going to do battle against evil.

All during the performance, Lynton kept looking up at Abby. Finally, while Ingrid and Channa did a dance to a Ennio Morricone tune, Lynton scurried up the escalator to find Abby. Seeing Lynton, Abby ran into her arms and cried, "I knew you would help me. I knew it."

Lynton whispered, "Of course I will help you, but I have to get back on stage. Is your mom with you?"

Abby replied, "No, that is why I am here. She is about to do something foolish. I need your help to prevent it."

Lynton, not wanting to leave Channa and Ingrid hanging, said, as she took Abby's hand, "Come on, we'll talk after the show."

As the three girls watched Abby down a big plate of spaghetti at Jollibee in the mall, they could not help but laugh at her rapid eating. Abby looked up and said, "You shouldn't laugh at a poor person eating like there will be no food left tomorrow, because tomorrow often brings more hunger to those who have nothing. I have known hunger all my life."

The precociousness endeared Abby to the girls, and as they got her another plate of spaghetti, they listened intently at how Abby felt that Reverend Augustus Haida was an evil man who was manufacturing miracles and making her mother fall under his spell. Ingrid was quick to interject, "I have heard Bradley talk about him, and Bradley sees nothing particularly bad in him."

Abby said, "No one but me seems to see the bad in him. Everyone is fooled by him, but you have to look inside him. This Bradley is like everyone else. He can't see beneath the surface."

Now Ingrid was genuinely enamoured with Bradley, and she took exception to anyone questioning his intelligence. Yet, she realized Abby was just a child, so she decided it would be childishness on her part to try and disprove her perception of everyone who did not question the Reverend Haida's integrity.

LYNTON WALKS ON WATER WHILE INGRID AND CHANNA DO AN IRISH JIG

Lynton handed Abby her cell-phone and insisted she call her mom, which she reluctantly did. When she finished, she handed the phone back to Lynton. Lynton assured her mom the three girls would gladly bring her back as they were planning on spending their week break between engagements in Taal anyway.

Ingrid, who was happy with the thought of going to a place where she could spend time with Bradley, enthusiastically agreed to go. Channa, who on the oterh hand, had plans with her boyfriend, but looked down at Abby's sad eyes and said, "The heck with my plans. Let's go to Taal."

Abby's mother was not angry with her at all so delighted was she to see her, but did say that punishment would have to be meted out. A sad Abby said goodnight to the three girls, and Lynton asked if she might tuck her in for the night. Pulling the sheet up over Abby, Lynton said, "Don't worry about the punishment. I can tell your mother is a good woman who loves you very much, and I can also assure you that I love you, and I, Ingrid and Channa are going to do what we can to help you. OK?"

LYNTON WALKS ON WATER WHILE INGRID AND CHANNA DO AN IRISH JIG

Abby managed a smile, and felt confident that Lynton was going to do what she could. She said, "I love you too Lynton. Thank you for caring. Guess what?

Lynton, quizzically replied, "What?"

"I have a big secret, and I think my secret is the reason that the Reverend Haida wants to marry my mom."

"You want to tell me about it?"

Abby motioning for her to come closer so no one could hear, said, "My daddy stole one million pesos from the bank."

Lynton said, "I know that Abby. That doesn't necessarily make him a bad person. I guess one way to look at it is that he was a thief who was stealing from other thieves, but that may be difficult for you to understand."

Abby, very seriously replied, "No, I understand that bankers are often just crooks in suits. My daddy explained that to me. However, I know where the money is."

LYNTON WALKS ON WATER WHILE INGRID AND CHANNA DO AN IRISH JIG

Lynton, weary of the implications knowledge of its whereabouts might cause, said, "Don't tell me Abby."

"OK, but I am scared of Reverend Haida."

Lynton, looking with earnest into Abby's eyes, said, "I will do all I can to help prove him a fake, and so will Ingrid and Channa. You can depend on us."

Now something else happened before Lynton left Abby, but that is not relevant at this point, so we will explore that later. As Abby slept the girls listened intently about the family's woes as Alana unburdened herself to the sympathetic girls, and, of course, shared with them the good news of her impending marriage to Reverend Haida.

The nest day, Lynton determined to investigate the so-called miracles that were attributed to Reverend Haida, while Channa and Ingrid made a trip to Palawan Prison to talk with the warden about Ben Ramirez to see if they might uncover anything unusual about his incarceration. It would probably lead to nothing, but the girls had learned through other investigations that truth was elusive.

LYNTON WALKS ON WATER WHILE
INGRID AND CHANNA DO AN IRISH JIG

Lynton's discussions with townspeople and members of the congregation led to nothing but lavish praise for the kindness, generosity, devoutness and holiness of Reverend Haida. No one had any unkind things to say about him. However, she ran into him downtown and introduced herself as someone who had heard good things about him, and someone who was desirous of attending services on Sunday. He invited her to the diner for lunch, and she cheerfully accepted, thinking it would be a good opportunity to get to know him better and get a sense of what type man he was.

Now, it is common knowledge that Lynton is a beautiful woman who exudes a generous amount of latent sex appeal, as has been alluded to earlier in her physical description. Sex appeal for most women is a concentrated effort on their part, but with Lynton, it is just a natural phenomenon. It is something that she is consciously unaware of, and when her boyfriend, Wayne, tells her how beautiful she is, her normal reply is "in your eyes maybe."

However, over the years she had become aware that men found her attractive. She actually got a kick out of teenage boys who would often, after passing her on the street, turn around and walk back by her to get another look. It was something she admitted to enjoying, as what woman does not enjoy knowing men find her attractive? Yet, she had no conceit about it, because she knew outer beauty was transitory at best, and that inner beauty was the true mark of genuine attractiveness. However, as she sat with Reverend Haida on this particular day, she noticed this reverential man of God who, no doubt, preached against sins of the flesh, kept glancing down at her breasts which, because of the blouse she had on, showed a generous bit of cleavage. OK she thought, he may be a minister, but he is still a man. That is no indication he lacks genuineness. However, his prurient interest did not end there. When they were parting after lunch, outside the café, he embraced her as people often do. Yet, the embrace lingered and he was obviously enjoying having her breasts push against his chest. This was no ordinary embrace, and Lynton formed the opinion that this was also no ordinary minister. Yes, there was definitely something sinister about this man.

CHAPTER 9
ABOUT TO BECOME DEADLY

Augustus Haida had asked for Abby's mom's hand in marriage, and the wedding was set for eight weeks time. Robert Torres' master plan was falling into place, and just to make sure things were running smoothly, he decided that he should broach the subject of the money with Alana for the first time. "Darling, I do not want anything to mar our love for one another, but I naturally have heard the rumours of you being privy to the location of that ill-gotten money that your dear departed husband so brazenly stole. It is an abomination that money, an abomination that stands between you and salvation if you know its whereabouts."

Alana was desperately in love with Augustus, but she still had loyalty to Ben, and simply was not ready to reveal where the money was. Maybe in time she thought, but now was not the time. "I do not know my dear. I was never privy to its location. He never trusted me with the knowledge, and he went to his death without revealing anything to me. It is ill-gotten money, and it is rotting in the ground I suppose."

LYNTON WALKS ON WATER WHILE INGRID AND CHANNA DO AN IRISH JIG

"I hope you are not lying my dear, because trust is important if we are to make this marriage work. By the way, why don't I take Abby and Louie to the movies this afternoon. I want to get to know them better, and prepare them for accepting their new daddy."

Thrilled that he was so interested in the children, Alana replied, "Of course. It is a wonderful idea."

She called in Abby and Louie, and Louie was excited about going, but Abby said, "No thank you. The only thing playing is the typical Hollywood junk. I prefer Filipino movies."

Augustus decided not to press the issue, because he thought getting Louie alone might be advantageous. Away from his sister, he might let his guard down. Maybe he knew where the money was hidden thought Augustus. Things were coming to a head, and he wasn't sure how much longer he could maintain his miracle persona among the people. Eventually, they might catch on. Right now things were going well, and he was skimming at least 5000 pesos (about $125) a week out of the collection plate. However, what he really wanted was the 1 million pesos. Then, he could high-tail it out of town and forget about the miracle scam, maybe even get out of the Philippines. Of course, he would also stiff his confederate, taking all the money and leaving him with none, but what could he do about it? If he revealed the truth, he would be arrested right along with Robert. Anyway, if his confederate caused too much trouble, the solution was murder. He had already done it once, so what was one more life in the endless sea of plenty thought Robert. Yes, things were falling nicely into place.

While Robert was at the movies with Louie, he casually mentioned as if it wasn't even important, while they crunched on popcorn, "So, your daddy hid a lot of money. I bet you can keep a secret. I bet you promised your daddy never to tell."

Louie had long ago forgotten his solemn promise to never reveal the whereabouts of the money he watched being hidden in Abby's stuffed doll, so he said without any conscious thought, "Yes, I can't tell. Abby would get upset with me if I did."

LYNTON WALKS ON WATER WHILE INGRID AND CHANNA DO AN IRISH JIG

Excitedly, Robert realizing he was close to getting his hands on the money, said, "Yeah, yeah, you don't want to get sis upset, but I can keep a secret too. Tell Augustus. That way you and I will have a secret we can keep between us. It'll be our little secret that we won't tell anyone."

Just then the movie started, and Louie said, "Later, let's watch the movie now."

Not wanting to spook the child and make him think he was too anxious, Augustus dropped the subject, and waited until after the movie, when they were having ice cream, to again bring up the subject. "So, Louie, let's talk about that secret. Tell Augustus where the money is hidden."

Just then, in walked Abby, who just overheard the word money, and immediately knew what Augustus was up to. She looked at him and said, "You're a crook. You don't love mommy, you love money." Then she took Louie by the hand and said, "You didn't tell did you?"

"No, no I didn't tell. I promise that I didn't tell Abby. I didn't. I didn't."

LYNTON WALKS ON WATER WHILE INGRID AND CHANNA DO AN IRISH JIG

Looking directly at Augustus, Abby said, "Remember, this man is evil. He wants daddy's money."

Fearful that the patrons would overhear them, Augustus whispered, "No, no, Abby, it is a misunderstanding. That is all, just a misunderstanding. Come, let me walk you two home."

Abby took her brother's hand and pulled him out of the ice cream parlour. The Reverend Haida kept pace with them, still fearful of what Abby might say to her mom. He decided that a good dose of fear might be better than playing coy. "Listen you little bitch. You say anything to your mamma about this and I'll cut both your hearts out while you are sleeping."

Abby looked up at him and said, "I won't tell. Mamma is too stuck on you to believe us anyway, but I warn you, stay away from me and stay away from my brother. I'm not afraid of you. Someone else knows about you and what you are really like. That person will protect me and my brother, even if my mamma won't. I am not afraid of you. I am not afraid of you."

LYNTON WALKS ON WATER WHILE INGRID AND CHANNA DO AN IRISH JIG

OK thought Robert. I need to lick my wounds right now. I know they have the money, and at the right time, I'll get my hands on it.

They parted company and Abby admonished Louie for his lapse of good sense. He promised to never tell, but he also could not understand why Abby hated the Reverend Haida so much. He said, "I like him. He's going to be our daddy. You shouldn't be so nasty to him."

She tugged at his hand and literally pulled him along. "Come on Louie. Come on."

While all this was going on, Lynton was busy talking to people around town about the miracles, and she immediately sensed that somehow Augustus Haida was simply manipulating people with slight of hand tricks that could be easily explained with time. The blood coming out of the wound simulated in the statue was an easy one, but making the sun dance was a bit more difficult to debunk.

One person even told Lynton, "This man can resurrect the dead if he wants. I know he can. He is God's chosen one."

LYNTON WALKS ON WATER WHILE INGRID AND CHANNA DO AN IRISH JIG

Meanwhile, as Ingrid and Channa sat in the warden's office at the Palawan Prison, they were getting an interesting picture of Ben Torres. Channa, as always, was meticulous in her diction and very precise with her words, which added to the warden's very obvious fascination with this alluring, charming, beautiful woman. Her questions were generalized as she was not convinced of the necessity of going to the prison as Lynton had insisted they do, because she did not see any connection between the prison and Augustus Haida.

The warden, enjoying the company of two beautiful women, was almost giddy when answering Channa's question about what type prisoner Ben Ramirez was. "Model prisoner in every fashion. The only trouble he had was with his cell-mate once. We considered separating them, but his cellmate, Robert Torres, was contrite, even apologizing for causing trouble. He took all the blame for the disagreement. We left them together, and Torres was with him when he died peacefully in his sleep. Torres woke up one morning and noticed he wasn't breathing. Torres was devastated by his death. You could see it edged on his face. Torres was released shortly afterward."

LYNTON WALKS ON WATER WHILE INGRID AND CHANNA DO AN IRISH JIG

Ingrid asked, "And Ben would never even hint about where the money was?"

Even though Ingrid's beauty was equal to Channa's, it was obvious that the warden was mesmerized by Channa, as even while he was answering Ingrid's question, he was looking at Channa. "Well, he was offered time-off if he would tell, but he never budged, never wavered at all. He just kept saying that bankers were worse thieves than most of the people in prison, and that the bank he stole from was insured anyway, so they lost nothing. It was the insurance company that was out the money, and they were bigger thieves than bankers."

After nearly an hour questioning the warden, Channa felt her strong protestations against wasting time visiting the prison were well warranted. However, just as the girls were about to leave, the warden offered a further observation, "There is one thing always bothered me though. You know Ramirez was sitting right there where you are Channa, talking to me and an insurance investigator one day when he said something that really has stuck with me. It was something that was so irrelevant."

LYNTON WALKS ON WATER WHILE INGRID AND CHANNA DO AN IRISH JIG

Channa, wanting to give the warden one last thrill, smiled provocatively at him, letting her luscious lips pucker right at the end of the smile, as she said "OK, what was the irrelevant words he uttered?"

Ramirez said, "Guess what? You people couldn't find a buried treasure with a precise map and an X marking he spot. What is in plain sight is often an illusion better than any magician could perform. Torres and his American buddy in the next cell are always trying to get me to reveal where the money is hidden. They don't realize that it is so well hidden that eyes cannot conceive its location, because we are blinded by the obvious."

Puzzled, the two were remiss in not pursuing things further. In fact, so upset at what she thought was a waste of time, Channa never even bothered to ask to see a photograph of Torres. Had she or Ingrid done that, the scams perpetrated by Torres and his confederate would have been immediately exposed, but Channa was not her usual astute self that day, and Ingrid, well, Ingrid had her mind on her date that night with Bradley Cooper, and was not listening as intently as she should have.

LYNTON WALKS ON WATER WHILE
INGRID AND CHANNA DO AN IRISH JIG

Of course, they were also unaware that Torres had bribed a clerk and had his photos destroyed, assuring no one would now what he looked like. The man was an srtist at deception.

Leaving the prison, the two women were so captivatingly beautiful that all the guards and administrative staff followed their graceful, gazelle-like strides that accentuated the sway of their bewitchingly seductive hips with stares of fascination. The click, click, click of their five inch heels was like a stake of seduction being pounded into the hearts of men who were titillated with desire.

Channa and Ingrid knew the effect they were having on the men, and they looked at one another with a sheepish grin of recognition. Yeah, the seduction game was fun, but back in Taal, sinister forces were at work, and that was no mere game. In fact, it was about to become deadly.

LYNTON WALKS ON WATER WHILE INGRID AND CHANNA DO AN IRISH JIG

CHAPTER 8

HE IS THROUGH

Let us now pretend to be T.S. Eliot in bloom, you and I,

When the evening is spread out against the sky

Like a patient etherized upon a table;

Let us go, through certain half-deserted streets,

The muttering retreats

Of restless nights in one-night cheap hotels

And sawdust restaurants with oyster-shells:

Streets that follow like a tedious argument

Of insidious intent

To lead you to an overwhelming question.

Oh, do not ask, "What is it?"

Let us go and make our visit.

In the room the con men come and go

Talking of the artist Michelangelo.

The yellow fog rubs its back upon the window-pane

The wickedness permeates like Abel being slain by Cain.

Licking its tongue into the corners of the evening

Lingering upon the pools that stand in drains,

Evil flourishes and causes such pains,

J. WAYNE FRYE

LYNTON WALKS ON WATER WHILE
INGRID AND CHANNA DO AN IRISH JIG

Slipped by the unwatchful, made a sudden leap,

And seeing that it was a soft warm night

Curled up with maliciousness and fell asleep.

And indeed there will be evil time

For the yellow smoke that slides along the street,

Rubbing its back upon the window-panes;

There will be time, there will be time

To prepare a face to meet the faces that you meet;

There will be time to murder and create,

And time for all the works and days of hands

That lift and drop a question on eternity's plate;

Time for the evil to take hold,

And time yet for a hundred indecisions

And for a hundred visions and revisions

Before the taking of a thing called hope.

In the room the con men come and go

Talking of the artist Michelangelo.

And indeed there will be time

To wonder, "Do I dare?" and, "Do I dare?"

Time to turn back and descend the stair

And lure the unsuspecting into their deadly lair.

J. WAYNE FRYE   160

LYNTON WALKS ON WATER WHILE INGRID AND CHANNA DO AN IRISH JIG

All outer confidence reflects an inner evil

That grows each day and asks, "Do I dare?"

Do I dare

Disturb the equilibrium of hope?

In a minute there is time

For decisions and revisions which a minute will reverse.

For this man Torres knows evil all;

He has known the evenings, mornings, and afternoons.

He has measured out life with coffee spoons;

He hears the voices dying but he will never fall

Beneath the music from a farther room.

So evil intentions he will presume.

His lying eyes already know deceit for fun.

The eyes that fix you in a formulated phrase,

And when he is formulated, sprawling on a pin,

When he hides his evil on a blind wall,

Then his horrid intentions begin.

He spits out evil and perceives it as no sin.

He laughs at those who have fasted, wept and prayed,

And mocks them with evil intentions

I am a prophet proclaims he, and therein lies the rub.

J. WAYNE FRYE 161

LYNTON WALKS ON WATER WHILE INGRID AND CHANNA DO AN IRISH JIG

He sees his moment of my greatness flicker,

And he has seen the glory in his own golden coat,

As he snickers behind the backs of his prey,

Letting them in ignorance lay.

He bites their pain with a smile,

To have squeezed the universe into a ball

To roll it toward some overwhelming question,

To say: "Rise Lazarus, come up from the dead,

For I am a false prophet, who on evil is fed.

I am what God meant me to be;

Am an attendant lord, one that will do

To swell a progress, start a scene or two

Advise the lame; no doubt, an easy tool,

Deferential, glad to be of use,

Politic, cautious, and meticulous;

Full of high sentence, but within obtuse;

Indeed, I laugh at your ridiculous reliance on miracles

that makes you such fools in my eyes.

I have seen my own evil riding on waves

cresting with my magical manifestations.

Ah, with your money I can afford Belgium lace

when the wind blows the water in my face.

J. WAYNE FRYE 162

LYNTON WALKS ON WATER WHILE INGRID AND CHANNA DO AN IRISH JIG

I have lingered in the chambers of the sea,

laughing at your reliance on miracles.

Can you not see each person makes their own miracles?

No, you sleep and let others think for you.

You shall see no blissful white in eternity.

You will lie on a bed that is dark brown,

Till human voices wake you, and you drown.

Love anything and your heart may be wrung with pain. Love is not always euphoric, but for Robert Torres (alias Reverend Augustus Haida) love was nothing but a game to play on the unsuspecting who desperately needed to know that there was something bigger than themselves, something that made them, although poor, somehow God-like. Seeing Reverend Haida perform miracles convinced them that there was hope. Yes, miracles happen. The person with cancer is cured, the lame walk, the blind see, and only the truly lordly had the power to perform those miracles, so the weak-minded saw the reverend as Godly.

Robert Torres saw most people as nothing but marks in the great con-game called life. He was at the top of the food chain, and his marks would always be at the bottom.

LYNTON WALKS ON WATER WHILE INGRID AND CHANNA DO AN IRISH JIG

People were all vulnerable and most lived in a fantasy world where good won out over evil. How naive thought Torres, because the ultimate victor was always evil. You couldn't pay your mortgage; the bank took your home. You couldn't pay your electric bill, the corporation turned off your lights. In many countries, you couldn't pay for medical care, the corporate hospital let you die on the hospital steps. Torres saw the real God as money. Without it in a world run by and for the wealthy, you were nothing, just a worthless piece of dung to be stepped over by the privileged class on their way to their palatial estates that were behind locked gates guarded by those entrusted to keep them safe from the riff-raff upon whose backs they accumulated their fortunes. That old adage, "without the poor, there would be no rich" is certainly appropriate, especially when you have people like Robert Torres to prey upon the less fortunate. Of course, Torres was small potatoes compared to the corporate con artists that convince dark-skinned Filipinos to buy skin lightener so they can appear whiter. The same corporation sells dark tanning cream in the USA and Canada, so white people can appear darker. Robert Torres was just another in a long line of con artists who saw no shame in scamming the gullible.

LYNTON WALKS ON WATER WHILE INGRID AND CHANNA DO AN IRISH JIG

Torres, like corporations, preyed mercilessly upon people's vulnerability by using fanciful fantasy and dreams to dangle before people what they thought was the good life. Yes, people must think happiness can be bought at the local mall, or in the local church where too many ministers like Torres see dollar signs sitting in the pews rather than people.

Lynton's brief time with Torres convinced her that the man was all fake facade with no depth of character. However, she knew what love did to women, and Alana was in love, so telling her about Torres' true character would probably be fruitless. Alana, like so many uneducated women, thought that a man was a necessity in life. For years, Lynton's friends had pleaded with her to leave a man whom she loved, but whom her friends saw as a leech and untrustworthy individual. In reality, men were often more burden than help. Lynton had learned that first hand by supporting her lover for nearly six years under the false impression that he desperately loved her and was trying to find that ever illusive job. One day when she caught him in bed with another woman in their own apartment, she let lose with a fury that was the topic of

LYNTON WALKS ON WATER WHILE INGRID AND CHANNA DO AN IRISH JIG

conversation for many months among her friends who knew her as such a demure, sedate, non-violent person. Her diminutive size, dignified and tranquil manner did not prevent her from standing against the emotional brutality of her lover.

Now, confronted with a large retinue of people who literally worshipped the Reverend Augustus Haida, she was contemplating the best way to expose the real man, so that all could see his true lack of character and his charlatanistic nature. As she sat and contemplated, she noticed it was almost six o'clock, and she prepared dinner for her and Channa, as she knew that Ingrid was going out with Bradley. Yes, it looked as if Ingrid had finally found that ever elusive man who would fill her nights with the affection she desired. Lynton was so happy for her. However, as the Ingrid would eventually discover, happiness can be a double edged sword.

Bradley was enthralled by Ingrid's beauty, and Ingrid found him to be a man who aroused deep passion in her. She was, however, exhausted from the day at the prison, but found him sympathetic to her plight, and also incredibly curious about what she and Channa found out, and what, if anything, it could possibly have to do with the Reverend Haida, who, after all, was a Filipino from the USA.

Ingrid, having decided, like Channa, that the whole day was an exercise in futility, said to Bradley with a tone of frustration, "I frankly think that Lynton is mesmerized by a child she fancies as being a lot like her when she was little. I believe that Abby Ramirez is just a little precocious child who has brought out the mothering instinct in Lynton. That is it pure and simple, but Lynton can be very stubborn. She has it in her mind that there is something nefarious about Reverend Haida. Hey, I am a believer, but I am a sceptic when it comes to any human being. The Reverend is just a man. That is all and men are fallible. We are all fallible. So he might be pretending to perform miracles. I have a doctor who every time he examines me thinks he is performing a miracle. Frankly, I think it is a miracle I get out of there safely because his solution to every illness I have is – take your cloths off and lets check you out."

Bradley laughed and said, "Well, I can see why he would want to do that, Ingrid. You have an incredible body."

LYNTON WALKS ON WATER WHILE INGRID AND CHANNA DO AN IRISH JIG

"Well, thank you Bradley. Yours isn't that bad either."

Again they laughed, and a deep sense of mutual attraction was obvious as they fawned over each other the rest of the night.

While Ingrid was out with Bradley, Channa and Lynton discussed the situation with the Reverend Haida. Channa was still perturbed, because of what she considered a wasted day. However, Lynton was beginning to connect the dots on a big, intricate puzzle. She very sternly asked, "I know the warden was probably enamoured with you two girls, but did you manage to get any concrete information on Ben Ramirez, anything that might somehow point to Reverend Haida. Perhaps Ramirez knew him or knew an acquaintance of his. I, along with Abby, sense that he is looking for that money and that all this miracle stuff is just fabrications to keep the collection plate filled while he is trying to locate it. Why he might even be a plant by the insurance company that had to pay-off the bank for the stolen money. Insurance companies and banks are just entities with a licence from the government to brazenly steal and plunder."

LYNTON WALKS ON WATER WHILE INGRID AND CHANNA DO AN IRISH JIG

Channa, her furtive mind beginning its contemplative process, sit up in her chair with her ramrod posture that protruded her chest and made men's hearts flutter, very methodically and precisely said, "OK, let's examine your theory. If the insurance company sent him, the company would not risk alienating so many people with a con game based on miracles. So, no, you are wrong, but you may be right about something else. You want a connection, a connection between Reverend Haida and Ramirez before the fact. I know your thought processes Lynton. With you, this is a linear progression. *A* leads to *B*, *B* to *C*, etc. and there are no curves or obtuse angles. OK, I can understand that line of thinking, although I am not sure it makes sense. I have never met the Reverend Haida, nor has Ingrid, but you have. Describe him, and what you think he is capable of. How far would he go to get money, and what is the connection you are seeking. You are holding back girl. I know you are."

"OK, here goes Channa. I believe that somehow Reverend Haida knew Ben Ramirez. Channa, this guy is one of the smoothest operators I have ever encountered, but he is no man of God. He proved that to me in the café."

LYNTON WALKS ON WATER WHILE INGRID AND CHANNA DO AN IRISH JIG

Channa, intrigued asked, "OK, so what happened in the café?"

"Channa, I admit this is an attractive man. He is tall for a Filipino, about 6 feet. He is about 35 and has a beautiful head of thick, black hair that is immaculate – not a hair out of place. His smile is disarming, and no doubt makes women fawn with desire to be kissed by his thin, but soft-puffy lips. His face is smooth and wrinkle free, and his body looks like it was chiselled by Michelangelo. His voice is so melodic and hypnotic that you hang on ever word. However, the eyes are the windows to the soul, and this man, believe me Channa, has no soul. There is an emptiness there, an evil lurking within."

Channa was intrigued, as Lynton continued. "Oh, those eyes could not be diverted from my breasts. He kept staring at them, longingly, as if he would commit any act, no matter how heinous, to see me topless. I have been ogled by men before, but never with the almost malevolent corruptness exhibited by this man, and under the table he kept brushing his leg against mine and it was absolutely no accident. He was aroused."

LYNTON WALKS ON WATER WHILE
INGRID AND CHANNA DO AN IRISH JIG

Lynton took a deep breath and continued. "And when we parted, he reached out for what I assumed was a friendly hug, but he grasp me and pulled me close to him, so close I could hear his fast-beating heart that betrayed his intense lust."

"Hey girl, you are beginning to sound like one of Wayne's books. I know it was traumatic for you, but frankly, I am a bit titillated. I wish you had gone to the prison, and I had gone to lunch with the hot Reverend. The warden is a bit too old, too fat and too boring for me. Besides, my boyfriend would feel better if I was with a reverend for lunch rather than a prison warden. Little does he know the reverend has a fireworks show in his pants."

They laughed, but it was only temporary euphoria. Lynton continued her train of thought in regards to Ramirez and Haida being acquainted. "I am sure the warden was sufficiently enamoured with you, as most men are, that he would gladly give you the current address of Ben's cellmate Robert Torres. Prisoners have to report their whereabouts while on parole. It is late, but call him now. Call him and ask the address. I tell you there is a connection somewhere here. We talk to Torres, and we will get a handle on this thing. I know it."

A phone call did not produce the results expected, as the warden said that Torres had simply disappeared without a trace. He was last seen on the ferry to the mainland. After that, he simply vanished. As for a picture of Torres, there was one taken upon his entry and his exit. Miraculously, they had both disappeared along with him.

Channa, a note of concern to her voice, said, "Why no pictures of Torres? What is it?"

"It is simple, very simple. Torres is doing something highly secretive, and no doubt, highly illegal. He had someone at the prison, whom he probably paid handsomely, to dispose of those photographs. Someone recognizing him would subject him to exposure. Does it have something to do with Ramirez and what is happening here? So, we now have a dual investigation. We must prove that this Reverend Haida is a fake, only out to procure that stolen money and to scam the people here, making them believe he can perform miracles."

LYNTON WALKS ON WATER WHILE INGRID AND CHANNA DO AN IRISH JIG

"So, what is out next move?" asked a puzzled Channa.

Lynton, concerned and perplexed, replied, "We go to that ferry. We know Torres was on it. He was seen. OK, call the warden and ask who saw him. We talk to that person and then we also decide how we are going to prove to Abby's mom that Reverend Haida is a fake. I've got an idea how to do that, but I will have to call Wayne and get his help, get some direction on how to proceed."

Channa, more eager and more convinced now of the righteousness of what they were doing, looked at the clock as it clicked to 3:10 in the morning. "Yeah, whatever we do, we'll have to do it without Ingrid. I think she is beginning to hear wedding bells."

They laughed, went to sleep, and after an early morning call to the warden found out that a crewmember named Tommy Lopez had talked briefly with Torres. They were off to the ferry that went from the mainland to Palawan. They were not keen about it, but enjoyed the sea breeze. They received a call from Ingrid in which she intonated that she thought Bradley was about to ask her to marry him."

LYNTON WALKS ON WATER WHILE INGRID AND CHANNA DO AN IRISH JIG

They were so happy for her, because they liked Bradley Ccooper, although they had only been with him briefly, and because marriage was something Ingrid had dreamed of. Being a wife was very important to her.

Now, talking to Tommy Lopez turned out to be an exercise in utter frustration, as he would not stop flirting with the girls. He kept telling them how beautiful, sexy and alluring they were, and how he had a friend who was on Palawan. They could all go out dancing that night and party hardy.

No matter how many times they told him they had boyfriends, he would just say, "What they don't know want hurt them. Come-on, you girls deserve real men, like me and my friend Harry."

Channa, in frustration said, "Forget it Lynton. This guy will give us nothing unless we give him what he wants and I am not partying on Palawan tonight or any other night without Mavs." She then looked at Tommy and said, "My boyfriend Mavs is enough man for me. Lynton, I'm heading up to the observation deck. You deal with this guy.

LYNTON WALKS ON WATER WHILE INGRID AND CHANNA DO AN IRISH JIG

Lynton acceded with a nod to Channa's decision and bade her bye, but of the three girls, Lynton was the most stubborn and tenacious. When Channa left, she said, "Listen, I don't cheat on my boyfriend, Tommy. However, if he says it is alright for me to go dancing with you, you have a deal. I'll call him and get his OK right now. You won't have that good a time, because frankly, I am pretty boring. Anyway, what do you say. If I get the OK, we'll do it next time I am out this way. I can't do it right now, because I am too busy working on this Torres thing. I am a woman of my word, though. My boyfriend says OK, and I will live up to my promise. You can count on that Tommy. OK?

Tommy wiped his brow, tilted his head downward, as if ashamed of his actions and said, "Hey, I just think you are hot. That's all. I just wanted my friends to see me with you, so I could impress them."

Feeling sorry for him, because she understood how all men liked to impress other men with their female conquests, Lynton smiled that gorgeous smile that lights up the darkness, moved a bit closer to him and said, "Hey, why don't I give you a little kiss when we get off the ferry in front of all your co-workers. You can tell them whatever you want about you and me. Embellish all you want."

Tommy puffed out his chest and said, "You'd do that?"

Shaking her head up and down slowly as she smiled, Lynton said, "Of course I would. You are a handsome man Tommy and very sexy. I am almost sorry I have a boyfriend, but I do. I am sure a handsome, virile man like you can understand my loyalty. If I was your girlfriend, you would want me to be loyal and true to you now wouldn't you?"

Ashamed of his behaviour to such a nice person, Tommy, acting a lot younger than his 19 years, said, "Yeah, yeah I would. Hey, I've been a jerk. I'm sorry."

Lynton's smile was the asset her boyfriend Wayne called "more valuable than gold." She flashed it broadly at Tommy as two deckhands walked by. She leaned over and kissed him very gently on the lips, so they could observe. Tommy was elated.

LYNTON WALKS ON WATER WHILE INGRID AND CHANNA DO AN IRISH JIG

Lynton did not have to ask, and as she looked up at Channa on the upper deck shaking her head in bewilderment at Lynton's finesse, Tommy was suddenly a bubbling fountain of information. "OK Lynton, so I can always tell the prisoners who just got out. There's a paleness too them from being inside so much. Knew this guy was freshly out of stir because of that. I didn't know his name, never did until the authorities from the prison interviewed all the deckhands when he jumped parole. This guy was a real dandy. I mean you could see he had a way about him, like he was somebody. Well, I knew he was nobody, because if you're somebody you get a high priced lawyer and don't go to jail, right? Anyway, I see him strike up a conversation with this other Filipino guy, dressed all in black with one of those round high collared shirts on. You know, kind of like ministers wear."

Tommy had to go no further. Lynton knew instantly. Robert Torres was Reverend Augustus Haida. He had assumed his identity and gone to the church posing as him. But where was the real Haida? Lynton looked down at the water, looked up at Channa and motioned for her to come down.

LYNTON WALKS ON WATER WHILE INGRID AND CHANNA DO AN IRISH JIG

She asked two last questions of Tommy. "You stand by the gangplank as the deckhand, making sure it is secure right? "

"Yes."

As Channa arrived, Lynton ask her final question. "You remember seeing the Reverend get off the boat?"

Tommy contemplated for a few seconds before replying in an almost startled fashion. "No."

Lynton gave him another kiss, turned and walked away with Channa as Tommy stood proudly on the deck while his crewmates were dumbfounded that such a mature and sophisticated lady would be kissing him. Lynton explained to Channa what happened. Channa, almost in shock, said, "You mean he killed the Reverend Haida?"

"At this point," replied a very cautious Lynton, "I cannot prove it, but when we get back to Taal, I am going to bring down the Reverend Haida or Torres, whichever, because he is a murderer or con artist or both, he is through!"

LYNTON WALKS ON WATER WHILE INGRID AND CHANNA DO AN IRISH JIG

CHAPTER 9

IT'S A MIRACLE BABY – A MIRACLE

Deceit you wicked bastard,

Creeping up uninvited,

No one sees you coming.

None will know when you are there.

Your delicious lies captivate and enthral.

And the ignorant fall prey

To miracles of the mind

While you play your game,

Dancing merrily in mischief and mayhem.

It is the imagination solely that performs all miracles. What in fact is a miracle? It is an exceptional phenomenon which is manifested in a pliable mind. Science leaves imagination to speak, which at once proceeds to invent and assert a cause out of all measure and proportion to the effect. The crowd accepts this assertion as gospel and the miracle is incontestable. Miracles are, in fact, nothing more than mental exaggerations. We read in the Bible that the mountains have leapt like rams and the hills like lambs? Must we take this literally or is it merely poetic licence? The unbending theologians contend that we must take literally the words of Jesus Christ when he says of bread, "This is My Body," and of the wine, "This is My Blood," but then is it not logical to take his words in a literal sense when he says "I am the true vine ye are the branches." Now was Jesus Christ truly and literally a vine? Must we believe that the knowledge of good and evil was really and truly a tree, and that the bitter fruits of this double-stemmed tree that yields life and death were apples? Could not the apple be a symbol, a representation of temptation that snares us in a web that tangles our minds and bodies in a captive commitment to allow others to think for us? Did a snake really communicate with Eve in the Garden of Eden or is merely an allegorical representation of all evil that crawls about in sliminess through lives that seem hopeless so often?

It is not the purpose of this book to explore theological explanations for what appears in the Bible or any other holy book, but the reader needs to understand that accepting everything at face value, without question is dangerous, because it places well-being in the hands of those who may have ulterior motives. Lynton saw what Robert Torres (AKA: Reverend Augustus Haida) had done to those

LYNTON WALKS ON WATER WHILE INGRID AND CHANNA DO AN IRISH JIG

simple people in the village who desperately wanted to believe that there was hope and that miracles were possible in lives that had been marginalized by an economic and social system that relegated the poor and disenfranchised to the periphery where they could observe the good life, but not in any way partake of it.

Men are often their own worst enemies; they love glory as the politicians love adulation; they go to seek it everywhere, even into hell, and turn around at the constantly to see if something is gaining on them. True glory is what none can take from us; it consists in merit, and not in the applause of the multitude; it fears not the caprices of destiny, because it owes nothing to chance; it loves neither tumult nor noise; it is in the silence of earth that we enjoy the peace of heaven. Lynton knew that, and she and Channa, while Ingrid was busy romancing Bradley, were preparing to do in the great charlatan who had so captivated Taal Heritage Village and captured the heart of Alana Ramirez.

That Sunday, a baptism was scheduled for the lakeshore and the Reverend Haida would be officiating. Lynton, and,

J. WAYNE FRYE   181

LYNTON WALKS ON WATER WHILE INGRID AND CHANNA DO AN IRISH JIG

if they could tear her from Bradley's arms, Ingrid, were going to prove Reverend Haida a fake.

Lynton had called Wayne and asked how she could fake a miracle. Wayne said that all she need do was called Chris Cooperman in Makati and tell him that "the marketing genius" wanted him to assist Lynton in performing a miracle. He owed Wayne many favours and would rush to Taal to aid her. Wayne encouraged her to let Chris come up with the miracle. Oh, and what a miracle it was to be. Chris enthusiastically suggested walking on water. He would need exact coordinates in the lake where she wanted to do it and he instructed Lynton how to get them. He would use a submersible vehicle and have a sheet of transparent plastic on top of it. All she had to do was walk off the boat toward a specific point on shore. However, she would only be able to take 8 steps because of the plastic's length, and then she would have to turn and walk back to the boat.

Lynton, a bit nervous said with a bit of levity in her voice, "Hey, there are sandbars in the Sea of Galilee where Jesus walked on water. Are there any sandbars in Taal Lake? I am not trying to outdo Jesus here."

LYNTON WALKS ON WATER WHILE INGRID AND CHANNA DO AN IRISH JIG

Laughing, Chris said, "Don't worry, just be far enough off shore where no one can see the submersible. We cannot be seen together as I am too well-known and people will immediately know it is a trick. Give me the time and date and the exact coordinates of a spot on shore. The night before I will have the submersible there and everything will be ready. I will send you a computerized sextant preset with the exact coordinates. Just push the button and you will be ready to perform a miracle. You still do dance routines with those sexy friends of yours?"

Lynton, worried but determined, said. "I'll be waiting, and thanks. Oh, yes, Channa and Ingrid are still dancers in the show."

"Now, I'd like to see them do an Irish jig while you are walking on water. What a combination. Hey, it would be an additional distraction to assure you are not exposed as a charlatan of illusion."

Lynton looked over at Channa and said, "You know Channa and Ingrid. They never miss a chance to dance and sing. They'll be there."

LYNTON WALKS ON WATER WHILE INGRID AND CHANNA DO AN IRISH JIG

That night, Channa and Lynton went over the plans with Ingrid, and pleaded with her not to tell Bradley. She flatly refused, saying, "He and I are going to be married. I am not going to start out a relationship and practice deception."

Now, remember that Channa and Ingrid had never met the Reverend Augustus Haida, but that afternoon, Ingrid, Channa and Lynton had been invited over to Alana's for afternoon tea at the suggestion of Abby, who wanted to find out what Lynton had discovered. Lynton and Abby went outside and Lynton, without telling her the plans for the next day, said, "You will see something unusual tomorrow at the baptism. I believe we are about to expose the Reverend Haida as a fake. Once your mom sees what he really is, you will have nothing to worry about Abby. He will be finished in this town. In fact, he will be going to jail for a very long time."

Abby looked up at her with tears in her eyes. "Lynton, you are my friend."

Smiling, Lynton looked down at her and said, "Of course I am."

LYNTON WALKS ON WATER WHILE INGRID AND CHANNA DO AN IRISH JIG

As the three women were preparing to go home, there was a knock at Alana's door. It was the Reverend Haida, who was very cordial as he was introduced to Channa and to a very, for some unknown reason, subdued, pale as a ghost Ingrid, who said, "Excuse me; I need to go to the comfort room (washroom)."

Ingrid came back in a few minutes. They all shook hands with the Reverend and left. Once outside, Ingrid said, "I have to throw up."

Mystified, as Ingrid went behind a bush to throw up, Channa and Lynton stared at one another and shrugged their shoulders.

Ingrid came out from behind the bush and said, "I have seen Reverend Haida before."

"What" replied Lynton?

"The first night Bradley took me out. Remember, I told you I saw him having a hated conversation. The man he was talking to that night was Augustus Haida."

LYNTON WALKS ON WATER WHILE INGRID AND CHANNA DO AN IRISH JIG

Suddenly, the pieces of the puzzle were falling into place. Lynton and Channa hugged Ingrid and said, "We are so sorry."

Wiping tears from her eyes and breathing deeply and sorrowfully, Ingrid said, "You damn right I won't tell him about our plans tomorrow. He is Augustus Haida's confederate. He is the man who has been helping him with the miracles. My guess is that if you check closely, you would find out he was in the cell next to Ben Ramirez and Robert Torres."

Lynton and Channa nodded their heads. Lynton was not one given to using profanity, but in this case, Ingrid and Channa knew she meant business when she said, "Let's nail these bastards."

Bradley was a bit put-off when Ingrid refused to see him that night, but he accepted the fact that she might be ill, as Robert had told him that she acted sick when he meet her at Alana's. Ingrid promised to see him the next day after the baptism. So, everything was now falling into place for a miracle Lynton style. The girls went to bed early as Lynton slept next to the sextant almost cuddling it. She imagined that Chris Cooperman was preparing the miracle so that the townspeople could understand that the man they revered was nothing but a money-grubbing charlatan. She recalled the story of another charlatan:

The fields were parched like cinders
The water had all dried up.
Then in rode a stranger bringing hope.
He looked up at the skies and said:
"I'm a rainmaker. I can make it rain."

He came to draught stricken town;
A saviour dressed in white with patent wet shoes.
He rode a horse that glistened as if touched with dew.
He said, "Something strange is in the air.
You can smell it. You can feel it."

He stared at the cloudless sky.
His nostrils flared as he sniffed.
He licked his finger and held it high.
There was moisture in the air he said.
"For a thousand dollars I will moisten your sandy sea."

LYNTON WALKS ON WATER WHILE INGRID AND CHANNA DO AN IRISH JIG

He showered the folks with watery tales,

But his deceit was well hidden.

There was solitude about him

As he made a kite soar

Across a barren sky.

At the core of this bravado

Was the foulness of deception.

People listened to his spiel.

Everyone is seen happily

slipping him a few bills.

And when he flees town,

You can hear his laughter in the hollow.

He stole the hearts of the women.

And from the men

He stole hard earned cash.

Back in town

The people look at the sky

Still hoping for a miracle.

But what they got

Was only a lie.

J. WAYNE FRYE

LYNTON WALKS ON WATER WHILE INGRID AND CHANNA DO AN IRISH JIG

Lies thought Lynton. Tomorrow the lies would be exposed, and the biggest miracle of all would occur. People would think for themselves and see that real miracles were not dispensed by the supernatural, but by kindness and compassion that rested in the hearts of those who had been abused by a system of greed where everything had a price.

On the shore that morning, Reverend Haida was stirring up the flock with spellbinding oratory. However, the gathered throng kept looking at a flat top rental boat about 100 metres off shore. On the sides was an advertisement – *Pinoy Boat Rentals*. Suddenly Irish dance music came blaring from the boat, and two beautiful women began dancing an Irish jig on deck while another one stepped onto the side of the deck, as if she was going to walk into the water. However, she did not walk into the water, she walked on it, and the crowd was aghast, turning their attention from Reverend Haida to the woman miraculously walking on water.

Lynton waved to the crowd, and Robert Torres signalled to his confederate, Bradley Cooper, to make haste and join him to go to Alana's home as, for some reason, she and the and the children had not shown up. Both men knew that their hoax had come to an end. They had to get out of town fast, but first there would be a stop by Alana's home, and the niceties were no longer necessary. Robert had his switch blade knife ready to do business. They were going to get the money.

As the boat came ashore, the crowd all flocked around Lynton, proclaiming a miracle. It was no longer Reverend Haida who was the miracle worker, but it was now the diminutive Lynton Viñas. Lynton stood on the shore and proclaimed loudly, "I am no miracle worker, and neither is Reverend Haida, who is, in fact, the killer of the real Reverend Haida, whose body lies in the ocean off the coast of Palawan. Your miracle worker is the con man, Robert Torres, and he made the blood flow from the wound on the statute with the help of a confederate who was behind the wall, and he made the sun dance with a giant mirror on the near side of the Taal Volcano, no doubt, also with the help of his confederate, Bradley Cooper. My miracle walk on water was achieved by a vehicle under the water and Plexiglas almost so invisible that you not only can't see it, but you cannot even feel it beneath your feet."

LYNTON WALKS ON WATER WHILE INGRID AND CHANNA DO AN IRISH JIG

There was a collective sigh of disbelief, but Lynton continued her homily ridiculing Robert Torres and Bradley Cooper and trying to point out that miracles were not the solution to problems. "I say to all of you, make your own miracles rather than expecting pie-in-the-sky in the sweet bye and bye. Stand up to authority. Do not just accept your lot in life with a shrug of your shoulders. Demand social and economic justice. Band together, because there are more poor than there are wealthy. There are more poor than there are government officials. There are more poor than there are police. There are more poor than there are corporations. There are more poor than there are banks. The poor, the disenfranchised united can be a mighty army of hope. Do not beg for fairness, demand it."

Lynton turned to Channa and Ingrid. "Girls, get the police and tell them to get over to the Ramirez home. I'm going there now to warn them. Channa, get a cab, I'm taking your car."

Lynton raced toward the Ramirez home, but while she was weaving through traffic, there in the home was Robert Torres, knife in hand. He had been told by Bradley Cooper, that the money had to be in plain sight, because he had been in the outer office when Ramirez said to the warden and insurance company representative, "Guess what? You people couldn't find a buried treasure with a precise map and an X marking he spot. What is in plain sight is often an illusion better than any magician could perform. Torres and his American buddy in the next cell are always trying to get me to reveal where the money is hidden. They don't realize that it is so well hidden that eyes cannot conceive its location, because we are blinded by the obvious."

Looking at the crying Louie and the frightened Alana, Robert was trying to be as sinister as possible to maximize their fear. He was brandishing the knife, and kept flicking it in and out of its sheath. However, Abby stood defiantly, exhibiting no fear whatsoever. Robert moved toward her and said, "Listen little bitch. Where is it? I know it is in plain sight. Let go of that damn doll and take me to it, or I'll gut your mom and brother."

Abby actually smiled and said, "Go ahead. You'll kill us anyway. You like killing. You think it makes you a man, but it actually makes you a coward."

LYNTON WALKS ON WATER WHILE INGRID AND CHANNA DO AN IRISH JIG

Robert gave her a backhand across the face and Abby went flying across the room just as Lynton walked in. Cooper shouted as the doll went flying across the room with Abby, "The doll. The doll. In plain sight. It's in the doll."

Lynton stood perfectly still, not moving a muscle, as Bradley Cooper held her at bay by pointing directly at her a butcher knife he had retrieved from the kitchen. Robert grabbed the doll and furiously began cutting into it. There was nothing but newspaper inside. Lynton smiled and said, "Gone jerk. She gave it to me the night I tucked her in bed, and the police will be here before you can get it. Work a miracle jerk. Come on."

Robert turned toward Lynton and said, "I may not get the money, but you'll still be dead bitch."

He furiously ran toward her, and as he did, Lynton pivoted to her right, raised her gorgeous dancer's legs with their muscular calves and kicked the knife out of Bradley's hand. Bradley lunged toward Lynton as Robert picked up the knife, but only managed to get in Robert's way as he lunged at Lynton and took the knife blade deep into his stomach.

As Robert pulled the blade from the dying Bradley, Lynton, like a panther leaping upon its prey, extended her right leg and gave a mighty kick to Robert's groin. As Robert doubled over in pain, he dropped the knife, which fell with the blade upright between Cooper's right arm and the right side of his chest. Screaming profanities, Robert tried to retrieve the knife, but as he grasped it with his right hand, Lynton rammed her high heel into his back. He fell on the knife, piercing his heart, and as he gasped for his last breath, all he could mutter was "damn. How'd a little broad like you best me?"

As blood gurgled out of his mouth, Lynton said, "It's a miracle baby – a miracle."

LYNTON WALKS ON WATER WHILE INGRID AND CHANNA DO AN IRISH JIG

EPILOGUE

BABY, I WALKED ON WATER

The police wrapped up things quickly. They did not know that the night Lynton was tucking Abby into bed, Abby had revealed that the money was in the doll. Lynton removed it and placed it under Abby's mattress.

She sat with Abby in her room going over the days events and letting Abby know how brave she was. Abby, said, "It was you who was brave. You saved our lives, Lynton. Thank you."

Smiling, Lynton said, "You are very welcome. Abby, I know your daddy told you to keep the money, and I am no fan of insurance companies, believe me. They are only slightly lower than banks on my list of offensive organizations. However, it is wrong to keep that money. I know you made a promise to your daddy, but sometimes doing the right thing means we have to break promises. There is a 10% reward if the money is found. They won't give it to you, because it was your daddy who stole it. Why not let me turn it in, and I will put the money in a trust fund for you and your brother."

"OK, Lynton. I will do as you want, because you are my friend.

"I am Abby. I am."

As the girls were driving home, Wayne called Lynton. She put it on speaker phone so he could talk to all of them, as he wanted to let them know how proud he was of them, but he had one question.

"Go ahead, baby. What's your question?"

"Well, when Chris called me and said he couldn't get the Plexiglas, I just wondered how you pulled off walking on water."

All Wayne could hear were gasps from all three girls, and Lynton shouting at him, "Baby, I walked on water."

**LYNTON WALKS ON WATER WHILE
INGRID AND CHANNA DO AN IRISH JIG**

DON'T MISS

THESE EXCITING

LYNTON ADVENTURES

By J. Wayne Frye

Lynton Curls Her Hair

Wayne Frye explores how a simple thing like a new hairstyle can cause vanity to rear its ugly head. Two parallel stories unfold, and vanity causes a night of terror in a small southern town while in the Philippines, love lifts the spirits of a very special young woman.

And

Lynton Buys a New Cell-Phone and Hears the Voice of Doom

A beautiful young woman buys a new cell-phone and starts receiving strange calls from a voice that leads her into a battle against demons in a haunted house.

**LYNTON WALKS ON WATER WHILE
INGRID AND CHANNA DO AN IRISH JIG**

Also

Available from Fireside

J. Wayne Frye's

Girl Series Books

The Girl Who Stirred Up the Whirlwind

**The Girl Who Said Goodbye
For the Last Time**

**The Girl Who Motivated
Murder Most Foul**

**The Girl Who Danced With
The Demons of Darkness**

**The Girl Who
Made Love to the Yeti
In Kathmandu**

And Meet the Woman Who Takes no Prisoners

**Chablis:
Avenging Angel for the Forgotten
In the City of Lost Hope**

LYNTON WALKS ON WATER WHILE INGRID AND CHANNA DO AN IRISH JIG

VOVACBULARY

Prologue

henchmen: trusted attendant, supporter, or follower.

animosity: strong dislike

vigilant: ever watchful

atrophy: wasting away of a part (usually body)

perpetrate: to continue, to go on, usually in a ill manner

scrutinized: examine in detail

morass: troubling or confusing situation

Chapter 1:

condemnation: a strong dislike

disparage: to belittle or discredit

deprecate: strong disapproval, belittle in a very harsh way

definitive: complete and total

sustenance: maintaining life, sustaining, nourishment

abominations: vile, shameful, detestable

equates: regard or represent

coveting: to envy or want something someone else has

nefarious: extremely wicked or villainous

charlatans: someone tries to fake knowledge or skill

oratorical: having to do with speaking

affirmatively: in agreement or positive reaction

modicum: a moderate or small amount

rotund: round in shape, plump

precocious: pre-mature development, actively knowing

gigs: slang for jobs, especially used by entertainers for jobs

grit: determination, devotion to accomplishing something

siblings: brothers or sisters

rudimentary: elementary knowledge of something

gruelling: very tiring or difficult

mêlée: confusion, turmoil, usually physical in nature

writhe: twist and squirm

ascribed: credited or assigned

fastidious: excessively critical or demanding

apropos: appropriate

sublime: complete and can be beneath the surface – not obvious

illuminati: enlightened ones who can do good or bad

J. WAYNE FRYE 199

derriere: the butt
epicurean: based upon the teachings of philospher Epicurus
Chapter 2
proselytizing: preaching and trying to convert
scrutiny: close examination or look
expendable: can be sacrificed
Hawthorian: having to do with Nathaniel Hawthorne
acerbated: embittered
aforementioned: what was said before
foray: quick attack or initial venture
permacious: European for unusual or out of ordinary
villainy: ill deeds
stead: useful to
charlatanistic: acting in a nefarious, ill manner
alluded: refer or make reference to
psyche: mental or psychological structure of a person
purview: range of operation or control
crux: vital or basic popint
discourse: communication or thought by words
tenacious: holding fast to convictions or job, won't give-in/quit
cantankerous: disagreeable
apropos: appropriate
heinous: hateful
impediment: getting in the way of
verboten: not allowed, forbidden
promulgate: proclaim/carry-on
debunked: exposed (usually for the good)
conundrum: anything that puzzles
omnipotent: unlimited power or authority (as God)
behest: command, directive or strong request
uproariously: very funny
chicanery: tricky or deceptive
Chapter 3:
fealty: obligation, faithful
admonitions: council, advise or caution
variance: varying, difference
repose: being at rest
perturbation: agitated or disturbed

tremulous: timid ort fearful
hitherto: up to this time
trepidation: fear, anxiety
perfidious: faithless, deceitful
imitative: (sometimes imitive misspelled) to do like
grungy: dirty, filthy, dilapidated
Chapter 4
precociousness: prematurely developed and very aware
astute: mentally sharp
simpatico: like minded
nefarious: very wicked
confederate: someone who assists you in a task
discombobulating: confused or frustrated
imbibed: to consume by drinking, soak up
perdition: spiritually wicked
conjugal: relationship (usually physical) between married people
suave: smooth acting with a lot of social skill
debonair: sophisticated charm
beseechingly: to beg or hardily implore
ardour or ardor: passionate, warmth of feeling
millennium: period of righteousness and happiness, 1000 years
tepidly: lack of force or enthusiasm
pique: to excite, arouse
broidered: to embroider or to complete a sewing
recompense: to repay or compensate
ruse: a trick
cottoned: wanted (colloquialism)
vassal: rendering homage as a means
refracts: to force back
synchronized: at the same time
Chapter 5
transitory: not lasting
fornicate: act of having sexual intercourse
banality: not fresh or original
Chapter 6
cadre: a group of trained people
placidity: calm, peaceful, unruffled
fortitude: mental or emotional strength

LYNTON WALKS ON WATER WHILE INGRID AND CHANNA DO AN IRISH JIG

enigma: puzzling or inexplicable occurrence
ravenously: intensely eager for satisfaction or to satisfy hunger
Pegasus: a winged horse for attacking
Hippogriff: mythical griffin with hind body of a horse
phosphorescence: luminous in appearance
conjurer: a person who conjures spirits or practices magic
prurient: lustful desires

Chapter 7

persona: persons perceived or evident personality
admonished: to caution or advise (usually against something)
debunk: expose as false or exaggerated
giddy: frivolous and light-hearted
contrite: filled with remorse or sense of guilt
protestations: declaration of objections or dissent
irrelevant: not applicable or pertinent

Chapter 8

etherized: render groggy or numb
obtuse: not quick or alert
deferential: respectful
adage: traditional way of expressing or observing
retinue: retainers in attendance upon an important personage;
charlatanistic: acting like a charlatan (deceiver)
fallible: likely to err, especially when being deceived
fawn: to worship someone as if they were important to you
periphery: edge or outskirts
partake: to take or have a share of
levity: lightness of behaviour
submersible: capable of operating under water
sextant: instrument to discover longitude and latutuede
spiel: high-toned talk or speech
jig: form of lovely folk dance
homily: short talk on a moral topic
brandishing: to shake or wave menacingly

DEFINITIONS TAKEN FROM CANADIAN OXFORD DICTIONARY

J. WAYNE FRYE

www.ingramcontent.com/pod-product-compliance
Lightning Source LLC
Chambersburg PA
CBHW070845120626
46556CB00002B/879